ISBN 13-978-0615543147

I0684904

This book is dedicated to my wife Kathleen

And to our children

PROLOGUE

Bright morning sun pierced the gothic stained-glass windows of the old Episcopal Church throwing cobalt blue, blood red and royal violet shafts of light bouncing off the slick ebony surface of the granite altar. The colors twinkled as if they were precious jewels spilled carelessly across black velvet; flickering candles nearby cast shadows of dancing ghosts across the walls and pews.

Solemn basso profundo notes rumbled deep within the church organ's copper and brass pipes, as if God himself stood nearby mumbling peevishly what a shame it was to have to bury the poor young man in the casket.

Twenty years ago I almost was that young man. But I had miraculously escaped death and now, here I was wearing my white vestments with black funeral sash, about to consign someone else to the grave.

Altar kids and lay people followed me in the processional to the altar. When we reached our destination my wife Ronnie smiled encouragement at me from one of the front-row pews. I turned to the congregation and announced that I would be performing The Burial of the Dead, Rite One.

"The grace of our Lord Jesus Christ and the love of God and the fellowship of the Holy Spirit be with you all," I intoned, raising my arms to bless Saint Paul's flock.

"And also with you," the congregation respond

"I am the resurrection and the life, saith the Lord. He that believeth in me, though he were dead, yet shall he live; and whosoever liveth and believeth in me shall never die."

"O God, whose beloved Son did take children into his arms and bless them: Give us grace, we beseech thee, to entrust this young man to thy never-failing care and love, and bring us all to thy heavenly kingdom; through thy Son Jesus Christ Our Lord, who liveth and reigneth with thee and the Holy Spirit, one God, now and forever, Amen."

How many times had I performed this ritual since becoming a priest? Hundreds I guessed.

Leading a Burial Mass was not one of my favorite things to do, but I felt an obligation to do it well. After all, if I hadn't survived blood poisoning, rheumatic fever and nearly drowning in the MacKenzie River, I would be dead.

Actually, Francis Albert Forsyth (that's me) did die, but God, in his infinite grace, allowed me to come back to life.

I remember that time as clearly as if it happened only yesterday. Sometimes though, it still feels like it's all just a figment of my imagination . . .

CHAPTER I

"Francis! Francis!"

"What?"

"Wake up!"

"Wake up?" Why?

"You're dreaming again," my mom said. "Turn that noisy radio off."

Dreaming? Again?

Well what else was a sixteen-year-old invalid nearly killed by blood poisoning then laid up for a whole year by the rheumatic fever supposed to do? It wasn't like my mom, who was trying to bring me back from near unconsciousness, was going to let me run outside and play baseball. I was so bored and frustrated by lack of physical activity I had to dream to keep from sinking into total depression.

Lately, my life felt like one huge disaster. A recurring dream I'd been having quite frequently was one where I was desperately trying to swim upstream against a flooding river, but the river kept clutching at me, sucking me down, drowning me in its mucky brown filth. It was a pretty scary dream. Little did I know at the time that I was having a serious attack of clairvoyance. If I had known, I might have begged out of that Christmas trip to my grandparent's house in Oregon.

People kept trying to encourage me, "Have faith Francis. You'll be your old self again before you know it. Maybe getting sick was a blessing in disguise. You never know how God might use something like this to focus your life."

Man, I hated it when they said that.

I figured if God was real; if he cared about me at all, it was time to give up already on the focusing and just let me have my life back the way it was before I got sick.

"Let me do things again God!" I would pray. I want to become a professional baseball player. I might as well pack it in if I can't play baseball."

Thanks, however, to rheumatic fever my shot at becoming the next Mickey Mantle seemed to be schlupping away faster than a plate of linguini at a Sons of Italy dinner (I made that up. Pretty good huh?)

Anyway, I didn't *feel* sick anymore. After six months at the hospital and six months flat on my back at home my heart *felt* fine. At my last checkup, my doctor said, "You're practically as healthy as a horse again. It should be safe for you to resume normal activity as long as you don't overdo it."

My mom, Mary Catherine McKenna, being the most stubborn and irritating Italian mother in the world, however, only heard part of what the doc said. She was convinced I would croak if she let me engage in any activity that required much physical exertion; especially if that activity involved the outdoors and especially when it had been pouring buckets of rain for days on end, like it was doing right now.

"You've got to be careful not to overdo," My mom reminded me. She had always been too strict, but since my illness, she acted like she was the warden of Alcatraz.

Yeah, I know McKenna isn't an Italian name, but trust me, my mom *was* Italian and she had the Latin temperament to prove it. She only got McKenna from marrying my stepfather Web. Granatelli was my mom's maiden name and she was as olive-skinned, doe-eyed-and dark-haired as Sophia Loren; only shorter, chubbier and not nearly as pretty. My mom did have beautiful long black hair and a soprano voice that rivaled any star of the opera (not that I liked opera). When my mom sang in church other people would shut up just to listen to her. Trouble is, most of the time my mom exercised her voice by yelling, not singing.

Being the oldest of eight kids I was usually the first one my mom yelled at. In fact, when my mom cut loose on me, her voice was so powerful you could hear her from one end of the block to the other. You know that saying, "It ain't over 'till the fat lady sings?" Well, the saying should go, "It ain't over 'till the fat lady yells." When my mom cranked her voice up to its full potential and yelled "Francis!" trust me, it was *over.*

She really ticked me off sometimes! I'm ashamed to say it, but I spent a lot of my hours in solitary confinement daydreaming of bad things happening to her so I could escape this prison I was in.

Ever since I started recovering from my illness, I'd start to ask her if I could do something fun and she'd say, "No."

"You don't even know what I was going to ask," I'd protest.

"Go ahead then ask," she'd say.

"Can I go outside and play baseball?" I'd say.

"No."

"Can I go over to Jimmy Foster's house?"

"No."

"Can I . . .?"

"No."

"But mom . . .!"

"The answer's no. Now quit asking."

"But you just said . . ."

"Never mind what I just said."

Her voice would be pegging at least eighty decibels on the Ear Drum Damage Meter at this point and I would be conjuring up a vision of a one-eyed, one-horned flying purple people eater (like in that song) dangling my mom in front of his huge stiletto teeth preparing to rip her apart for lunch. I liked that image a lot.

"If you eat her you have to keep her down," I warned the dragon. "No upchucking allowed."

My mom was flailing at the dragon with her fists and yelling at me, "You're not taking one step out of this house until I know you're not going to have a relapse."

"I'm not in danger anymore," I argued. "The doctor said I was fine."

"The doctor said not to overdo it. What about not overdoing it did you not get Mr. Smarty Pants? I'm your mother and I say you're not fine 'til the doctor isn't worried about you overdoing it."

She'd be hitting ninety decibels on the Ear Drum Shatter Meter now and I'd be visualizing her tied to a train track while Old Smokey Number 99 bore down on her hard and fast. Or I might conjure up an image of her jamming on the car brakes while rounding a sharp curve on a steep hill, and the brakes didn't work . . .

"I might as well die and get it over with," I'd grumble.

"Francis Albert Forsyth, it's a miracle from God that you are still alive and you blaspheme like that! You know we can't be too careful."

Where'd she get that *we* stuff? This was my life she was talking about. But her voice was pushing against the top end of the Ear Drum Damage Meter now, threatening to bust the red bulb at the end wide open. At the very least she might seriously strain something vital. Even though I had now conjured up a gleefully wicked scenario about stuffing her into a Safeway shopping cart and pushing it onto a major highway, I decided to back off. I couldn't beat her.

When I wasn't daydreaming of bad things happening to me or my mom I was daydreaming of good things happening; good things like me hitting the winning home run in the World Series, and a pretty girl calling me her hero – cool stuff like that. Trouble is, the good dreams were coming less and less frequently. They were being replaced by too many bad dreams – like drowning and other nightmares.

"If my heart has to quit on me why can't it quit while I'm doing what I want to do?" I asked looking skyward.

Instead here I was sitting around on my rear end waiting for God to *focus* me, and I was handcuffed to Gina Lola Grumpida the Italian Mother Hun. I was locked in purgatory or that Inferno place or wherever the heck I was, because I had been unlucky enough to come down with rheumatic fever. Lucky for my mom I was practically a saint - loving, kind, obedient . . . (you buying this?) or I might have dreamed up something really despicable happening to her.

Besides daydreaming, the only other avenue of escape from my dull boring life and my suffocating mom, until God answered my prayer or a nuclear Armageddon occurred - whichever came first - was to lose myself in reading a book. Fortunately, I liked to read and my mom had surprised me earlier in the week by checking 'Round the Bend out of the library for me.

'Round the Bend was a novel by Nevil Shute, one of my favorite authors. Mr. Shute quoted Emily Dickinson on the inside flap of his book. "There is no frigate like a book to take us lands away."

If only that were so! I felt like I was on a slow boat to nowhere - with violent squalls on the horizon.

Nevil Shute also had written a book titled *On the Beach*, which I read while I was in the hospital. *On the Beach* was a really scary story about these Australian people trying to cope with the after-effects of a nuclear war. The Australian people knew they were doomed to die from all the radioactive fallout circling the globe, but they carried on as if they didn't have a worry in the world.

"We're none of us going to have time to do all that we planned," one of the characters said. "But we can keep on doing it as long as we can."

I felt like I was doomed to die without even having the chance to do what I wanted to as long as I could.

A movie of *On the Beach* had starred Gregory Peck, Ava Gardner, Fred Astaire and Anthony Perkins. The movie was a pretty big hit. In 'Round the Bend" an Englishman named Tom Cutter realized, while watching members of a flying circus perform aerial stunts, that aviation was his life's ambition. The story took place between World War I and World War II and followed Tom's adventures as he progressed from fledgling pilot and mechanic, to owner of a successful air freighting business.

Like I said before, my big ambition was to become a famous baseball player. I wanted to play centerfield for the New York Yankees, like Mickey Mantle, and hit home runs and be famous. My mom wanted me to become president of the United States (like I had a chance at that). Worse yet, my grandma Granatelli wanted me to become a priest. Grandma figured since God had saved me from the rheumatic fever, I owed it to him.

"I can just see you in a Cardinal's red vestment," grandma would say.

Grandma's eyes would moisten up and she would thank the Virgin Mary and kiss her rosary beads. Then she would look at me and sigh hopefully, like I personally could open the pearly gate to heaven for her if I became a priest.

The nurses at the hospital, other family members and friends, even people I didn't know, annoyed the heck out of me too by constantly reminding me of the debt I supposedly owed to God. It was like a religious conspiracy. The scary thing was, deep down in my heart, I was afraid maybe my grandma and all those other people might actually be right. Then what? I was pretty conflicted.

Cardinal Francis Albert Forsyth did sound pretty cool. And I had *said* more than once that I was willing to do anything if my life would change. But I also wanted to enjoy life. I didn't want to take the vows of a priest if I didn't have to.

My sister Loretta once mistakenly called a Cardinal's red vestment a red jacket. I was afraid the Cardinal's vestment might become a red straight jacket if I ever put it on. No way could I hope to be good enough to bring honor to the priesthood. I didn't *want* to be that good; especially good enough to become a cardinal. No matter how hard I tried, I couldn't even stop wishing bad things would happen to my mom.

I struggled to picture myself walking around in a Cardinal's vestment, swinging one of those incense thingies, being all holy and blessing poor unfortunate souls. But I usually lost that struggle.

Besides, what about girls? I read that Roman Catholic priests had to be celibate. I knew what celibate meant and I didn't like it one bit. If you were celibate you didn't get to kiss girls and fall in love. That was a hard and fast rule. Sure, priests helped poor people and prayed for their salvation and performed good deeds among savages in the jungles, and really, who could aspire to a better life than that? But, no girls? No falling in love? Not for me thanks! I liked girls.

To tell the truth, I fleetingly considered becoming a millionaire playboy if baseball player or cowboy actor (my other career choice) didn't work out. Millionaire playboys had lots of girlfriends. I could picture myself as a sophisticated man of the world; driver of fast cars; lover of beautiful women; daredevil adventurer.

I overheard Sally Bastion, one of Loretta's friends, say to Loretta one time, "I hope Francis didn't come down with romantic fever because of me; instead of rheumatic fever. But maybe Sally had something there. Maybe I possessed a little Casanova blood in my veins. I could see me giving that famous Latin lover a run for his money.

Lucky for me, my mom had rebelled against Roman Catholicism and had married the son of a Baptist preacher (that's why my last name was Forsyth).

She didn't stick with my real dad very long and I didn't even remember him, but because he was Baptist, I was supposed to be Baptist too or at least some kind of Protestant, certainly not Roman Catholic and certainly not a Roman Catholic priest.

"I am adamantly opposed to Francis taking the vows of a Roman Catholic priest," my mother told my grandma. And that was the end of that argument.

Even if I struck out as a major league baseball player, or didn't possess enough machismo to succeed as a millionaire playboy or couldn't sit a horse well enough to ride off into the sunset like Roy Rogers or Gene Autry, I figured I could think of *something* better to do with my life.

The only thing worse than becoming a priest and dedicating my life to poverty and celibacy and no girls would be selling my soul to a sawmill like my stepfather Web.

"You don't want to wind up working in a saw mill like me," Web had once warned me, and as far as I was concerned, he was right.

Worst-case scenario – I might conceivably be overcome by the Holy Spirit and turn into a Bible-thumping, fire and brimstone evangelist or something totally weird. But at least I wouldn't have to become a priest and take a vow of celibacy and give up girls. Ever since that wonderful night at the eighth-grade graduation dance with Candace Reulmann I was pretty sure I couldn't resist falling in love.

One thing concerned me about girls and falling in love though. I hadn't felt anything physical happen to my heart when I was struck down by rheumatic fever. It just sneaked up on me and wham! One day I was walking around school looking cool in my new Florsheim wingtip shoes, the next day I was carted off to the hospital.

If falling in love was like rock-and-roll singers and famous novelists described it, it was like being struck by lightning or being whacked in the head by a high, hard fastball. In theory, love shouldn't be able to sneak up on a guy. But was that true?

I sure didn't want to end up like poor Tom Cutter. He started a successful aviation business and was living fat, dumb and happy, then pow! He didn't see love coming, it nailed him, next thing you know, he fell for a girl and got married. Unfortunately, the marriage didn't last. After a few years, Tom's wife dumped him and ran off with another man. Poor Tom didn't see that coming either. Tom blamed himself for the divorce.

"You can only do a thing for the first time once, and that goes for falling in love," he said. "You may do it over and over again afterwards, but it's never the same. When you chuck away what's given to you that first time, it's chucked away for good."

When I really thought about it, I had to admit that taking the vows of priesthood might be safer than falling in love. I had to acknowledge that possibility. Still, I couldn't help reasoning, "If rheumatic fever is the worst thing that could happen to me, and it hasn't killed me, falling in love can't either."

If I ever was allowed to live normally again I intended to prove it. I had absolutely no intention of becoming a priest.

CHAPTER II

Near the end of my first semester as a freshman at Portola Union High School – November to be exact – was when the rheumatic fever nailed me. The way it happened was so weird.

Usually every summer, before a new school year started, my mom would take all of us kids to the shoe store and buy each of us a new pair of shoes. Those shoes were expected to last the entire school year. Sometimes they did, sometimes they didn't. But Web was laid off from his job right after my graduation from eighth grade.

"There's no money for new shoes," right now, my mom said. So I started high school without new shoes.

There was no money until October when Web finally was called back to work. I'd had to skip turning out for JV football because we couldn't even afford the five dollar fee for athletic insurance. That had been a bitter pill to swallow, but it wasn't Web's fault. I knew that and I just had to buck up and face facts. In October, my mom said, "I think I can squeeze enough money out of the family budget to buy you a pair of those black Converse sneakers if you want."

"I don't want sneakers mom!" I protested. "Kids who wear sneakers to school are poor."

I did not want my classmates to think I was poor. No doubt they already knew, but I didn't *know* that they knew and I wanted to keep everybody in the dark as long as I could; including myself. So I refused the new sneakers and held out for a pair of wingtips, which my mom promised me she could buy in November.

The first week of November, as soon as Web's paycheck was deposited in the bank, mom took me to Jordan's Fine Bootery in downtown Fern Valley and bought me Florsheim black wingtips, size twelve triple E.

"My gosh," she told Web afterward, "The boy has the feet of a full-grown man already and he's not even fifteen years old. How big you think his feet will get before he's done growing?"

Web said he didn't know the answer to that. Pretty big though, was all he would hazard to guess.

"Those shoes cost twenty five dollars," my mom said. "His hooves are so huge it cost more than two dollars a foot to shoe him. Might as well be a horse."

"Big horse," Web said. "All that leather. Clydesdale maybe."

I was somewhat embarrassed about the fact that it cost so much money to buy my new shoes. I did know times were tough for the McKenna family and that money didn't grow on trees and I couldn't help feeling just a little selfish. Still, I couldn't resist strutting around some in my new twenty-five dollar shoes. They sure were a lot higher quality than ten-dollar Converse sneakers. My shoes even cost more than Loretta's shoes. Life didn't get much better than that. Anytime you could lord something over on your little sister it was worth the price.

My shoes had genuine leather soles with little triangular wedges of hard rubber in each heel. I guessed that was to keep the heels from wearing down too fast. I considered asking my mom if I could have taps put on the heels to protect them further, but decided I would make too much noise walking down the school hallways. I did not want to attract a lot of attention to myself as a lowly freshman.

So, first thing next Monday morning, I strutted off to high school wearing my new wingtip shoes. Even though they were brand new, I had shined them until they nearly blinded me to look at them. I might not want to be noticed, but I sure wanted my new shoes to be noticed. Unfortunately, about halfway through the school day my right shoe started to rub a blister on my heel. By the end of the day, I was sporting a painful, angry, pussy red blister and I still had to walk home.

I limped home, took my shoes off, popped the blister and ran outside barefoot to play baseball with the neighbor kids.

But I didn't last long. Before my mom even called me in for dinner, my right leg got all hot and achy and it looked like there were red streaks running up it almost to my knee.

I suspected I might have a problem, but boy! I did not want to tell Web and my mom. If we didn't have money for a new pair of shoes, we sure didn't have money to take me to a doctor. I was going to tough it out and hope my little problem would go away. Too bad I made the mistake of confiding in Loretta that I was worried about my leg. I knew better.

How many times had I told myself, and anyone else who would listen, "Never tell Loretta anything; she is nothing but a big blabber mouth and your secret will be spread all over kingdom come before you know it?" No sooner had I confided in Loretta than she told my mom, "There's something wrong with Francis' leg."

Sure enough, my mom came after me wanting to know what was wrong with my leg. I probably owed my survival to Loretta, but I'd be darned if I'd ever admit it. I also reserved the right to be ticked off at her the rest of my life if I wanted. Anyway, as soon as my mom saw my leg she said, "Oh my gosh, you've got blood poisoning."

"Is blood poisoning serious?" I asked stupidly as mom dialed the telephone to call a doctor.

Of course it was serious. The doctor told my mom to bring me to his office right away. By the time we arrived at his office I was feeling really bad. I could tell I had a temperature, and a pretty high one. In fact, I felt like I was burning up.

The doctor gave me a shot of something and sent me home with adamant and worried instructions to my mom.

"Pack his whole body in ice and don't waste time doing it," the doctor said. "You've got to get his temperature down as quickly as you can. If he goes into convulsions, it'll be touch and go."

I don't remember much after that, but my mom told me later that I did indeed go into convulsions shortly after we arrived back home.

She and Web had packed my body in ice as instructed, but my temperature shot up to a hundred and six.

You nearly died Francis," my mom told me. "Me and some people who came from church prayed all night and laid hands on you and everything."

The next morning, I woke up feeling like I'd been run through the ringer, but judging from the look on my mom's face, I knew I had dodged a bullet. When she told me she and Web would be taking me back to the doctor that afternoon, I didn't sweat it. I figured I would just get another shot of magic drugs and a warning to be more careful about blisters.

Boy was I wrong! After taking my temperature – yeah, with a rectal thermometer (sliding that greasy thing up my backside) - thumping my chest and looking down my throat, the doctor pulled mom and Web outside the examining room for a whispered conference.

When they all came back in the room, they looked at me real serious like and the doctor told me, "We need to send you to the hospital for some tests Francis."

Tests didn't bother me. I figured that was pretty routine. I'd submit to a few tests then I'd go home. Wrong again!

At the hospital, after submitting to chest x-rays, more chest thumping, more looking down my throat – and yes, another Vaseline-greased rectal thermometer – I was informed by a nurse, "We're going to have to keep you at the hospital overnight."

I didn't like that idea at all, but mom and Web gave me no choice. Then they lied to me and promised me they would pick me up in the morning and take me home. The nurse ordered me to take a couple of white pills the doctor at the hospital prescribed for me. Next thing I knew I had drifted off to la-la land. Oh, what a weird dream I had that night! I dreamed I was crawling around the walls of the hospital like a giant scaly lizard. Only I wasn't a lizard, I was me. I thought it was pretty neat to be able to stick to the walls like that though.

The only drawback was that I was wearing one of those nightgowns they always make you wear in hospitals; you know, the ones that gap open about four inches in the back so your naked behind is hanging out there for the all the world to see? I'm pretty sure mine was hanging out.

Anyway, I was crawling around the hospital walls and I was pretty scared because I heard someone moaning, obviously in serious pain.

"Oh-h-h. Oh-h-h."

At first I thought the moans were coming from ghosts, because the wind blowing through an open hospital window moved the curtains in a way that they looked like ghosts. When I realized the moans were coming from me I figured I was dead or dying and the ghosts were coming to take me away. I wasn't ready to pal around with ghosts yet so I said, "I'm outa' here," and slipped out the window.

Next thing I knew I was tripping down this long, long, *long* spirally tunnel, kind of like the one in *Alice in Wonderland*. After several minutes of alternately walking a few steps, falling down, drooling and giggling, I landed on my knees in a dark mossy place. Then a thought occurred to me.

There might be snakes in the here!" I was afraid of snakes.

I felt like upchucking my dinner. Then, through glassy, unfocused eyes, I noticed a light, way, way, way down at the end of the tunnel and I started crawling towards it.

I don't know how long I crawled. I was so dizzy and nauseous, it seemed like forever. I even considered just laying down up and going to sleep and never getting up again, but something compelled me forward. Eventually, I arrived at what appeared to be the end of the tunnel. I say that because I was looking at a thick oak door –at least I guess it was oak – with a big brass knocker on it.

I managed to pull myself upright and searched for a handle to open the door, but there didn't appear to be a handle, just the knocker.

I took hold of the knocker. Feeling very weak in the knees, I somehow managed to pull myself up a little straighter and bang loudly on the door.

"Help! Let me in," I croaked.

Then the knocker turned into one of those bells you see on motel desks. Weird. Just as I was about to hit the bell with the palm of my hand to make it ring, it turned into a frog that croaked "ribit." For a minute nothing else happened. Then, just as I was getting ready to pass out, the door slowly creaked open. A bright shaft of light spotlighted a path in a forest. The forest looked a lot like the forest at South Fork Mountain where Web and I used to hunt deer. But I didn't see any deer. What I saw was Jesus.

I'm not kidding!

There was no doubt in my mind whatsoever that the man seated on a large redwood stump in the forest clearing was Jesus. I figured this was it, the jig was up. I had been summoned to judgment for all my sins. That straightened me up real fast!

Jesus looked just like the guy in the picture hanging over my grandma's bed. He was lean and muscular like a carpenter alright. He was wearing brown leather sandals, a glowing white robe, a red cape and a crown of thorns. I could see nail holes in his hands. He searched my eyes as if he were looking straight into my heart, then suddenly I could read his thoughts.

"You're tired, come rest your head in my lap," he said.

Let me tell you, I really, really wanted to rest my head in Jesus' lap. I felt more tired than I'd ever felt in my life and I knew somehow that laying my head in Jesus' lap would be the most relaxing, soothing thing I could ever do. My legs felt as heavy as lead weights though. And my head throbbed. I had absolutely no strength to move any part of my body.

Jesus beckoned me again. "Come," he said.

Next thing I knew I was floating toward him. I think I was having one of those out-of-body experiences. It was then that I noticed my hospital gown had turned into a pure white robe – just like the fleece of a lamb.

"Am I dead?" I asked Jesus. I admit I was a little bit afraid.

"Are you ready to come live with me and my father in heaven?" Jesus asked.

"Boy, I don't know," I said, figuring I better tell the truth. I mean, Jesus would know if I was lying, right?

"You don't have to come," Jesus said. "You can go back if you want."

Now I was in a quandary. I really wanted to lay my head on Jesus' lap. The desire to feel his comforting caress, to have him pat me tenderly on the back was so-o-o tempting. All the things I'd learned in Protestant churches about heaven – streets of gold, a castle for my home - that sort of thing - made me really want to give in to the temptation. Still . . .

"It's okay if you want to go back," Jesus said again.

I should have known he could read my mind too.

"I don't mean to seem ungrateful," I said.

"Not at all," Jesus said. "We're giving you the option. The decision is strictly up to you."

"I'm only fourteen and I would like to play professional baseball and get married someday," I explained. "I might even become a priest, you never know."

"You shall do what our Father has planned for you," Jesus said.

"Maybe baseball is your calling, maybe the priesthood. Remember, faith is the assurance of things hoped for . . ."

"And the conviction of things not seen," I said. "I know. You sure it's okay to go back?"

"It's okay," he said.

A breeze came up then. It was a cold breeze. It felt like it was going to rain and I shivered.

"Just like the weather in the mountains to change so quickly," I thought. "I should have brought a jacket."

Jesus untied his red cape and threw it around my shoulders.

"Wear this," he said. "It will warm you, protect you and give you courage."

I suddenly had this weird feeling I was wearing a red cardinal's vestment, but I also felt a new wholeness course through my veins. I was going to be okay!

"Wow thanks!" I said, feeling a little spooked and wondering if I was showing enough gratitude.

"Bless you Francis Albert Forsyth," Jesus said. "Because you believe in me my father's holy spirit is with you."

Then he was gone and I was back on my knees in the tunnel.

The oak door had closed behind me and the light was fading. I felt an urgency to run somewhere because my legs suddenly became wondrously strong – but to where?

Back to the hospital as it turned out. When I woke up in the morning my mom and Web and a doctor stood at my bedside.

"Can I go home now?" I asked. "I feel great."

No, I couldn't go home.

"You have rheumatic fever Francis and you're going to have to spend some time in a children's hospital in Santa Rosa," my mom said.

"How much time?" I asked fearfully. Santa Rosa's nearly three hundred miles south of here."

"We don't know," mom said.

"Is rheumatic fever like polio?" I asked. "Will I be crippled?"

I didn't say anything about Jesus telling me in my dream that the Holy Spirit would protect me. My mom wouldn't have believed me and my dream probably was drug-induced anyway. I noticed that I wasn't wearing the red cape Jesus gave me, so obviously, I had been dreaming

"Rheumatic fever affects your heart," the doctor explained. "The blister on your heel broke open and was infected by bacteria – streptococcus we call them – which led to septicemia or blood poisoning. The bacteria are on your skin all the time. Blood poisoning resulted in the streptococcus flowing into your heart. You may have a damaged valve, which could seriously affect your future health, but with the right care, you should eventually be as good as new.

Eventually? How long was eventually? I might as well have been given a death sentence.

"You said you were going to take me home this morning," I wailed at my mom.

I looked at Web, accusing him of betrayal too. I didn't dare look at my mom that way because she would have whacked me, rheumatic fever or no rheumatic fever.

"We can't take you home just yet Francis," mom said.

Wailing didn't work, so I tried anger.

L yelled as loud as I could, "This is totally unfair! I didn't do anything to deserve this."

I tried cajoling. I promised I would be on my best behavior if I could just convalesce at home. I tried crying. Nothing worked. I was bundled up, driven to Santa Rosa and dumped at the children's hospital - abandoned. I would spend the next six months in that hospital wondering what was going to become of me.

CHAPTER III

It was now December twenty first, nineteen sixty four, four days before Christmas. Since my mom made me turn the radio off and I didn't have anything else to do, I curled up on the living room couch, turned my back on the wet gloom outside and tried to read another chapter of *'Round the Bend*. Unfortunately, I just couldn't concentrate. I really wanted to go to Oregon to visit my grandma and grandpa Granatelli for the holidays, but the weather was not cooperating.

Nineteen sixty four was a season of massive flooding in Northern California, Oregon, Washington and Idaho. It had been pouring rain almost non-stop for thirty days and thirty nights. Rampaging rivers and creeks had already killed five people and left several others missing. The dead included a sixteen-year old girl in Medford, Oregon, who fell into a swollen creek and was swept away. The girl's father was killed when he jumped into the creek in a futile attempt to save her. Two old ladies met their maker when their car plunged into a river near Sandpoint, Idaho. And a man had drowned while trying to dynamite a log jam on a rural Washington state river.

I even read a story in the newspaper about a bunch of dairy cows that were killed when flood waters swamped their barn. The people who owned the farm camped out in the hay loft of the barn for a couple of days trying to stay above the water.

"We had to listen to our cows drowning all night long," they told a newspaper reporter.

I had always thought cows could swim, like horses, but maybe not. Maybe the barn was locked and the cows couldn't get out even if they did swim. I could only imagine how horrible knowing they were going to drown must have been for those cows. I imagined them straining to keep their noses above the rising water as long as they could, mooing frantically for help that never came. If they could swim, they probably swam around in useless circles until they ran out of strength.

If the farmers listened to their cows all night long, some of the cows must have lasted a long time - only to perish in the end.

I was convinced that drowning would be a terrible way to die; straining to catch your breath while water flooded into your mouth and down your throat, choking the life out of you. It certainly seemed like a worse way to go than dying from convulsions brought on by blood poisoning. At least when I had blood poisoning I didn't know I was dying. I just had a weird dream.

"I would probably panic like most people if I were drowning," I thought.

I preferred to die displaying a little more dignity. All in all blood poisoning didn't seem like such a bad way to go. Rheumatic fever might be an even better way to go. One day your heart just stopped working.

But I didn't really want to die, at least not yet. I had been given a reprieve and I wanted to make the best of my opportunity; if I ever got the chance.

A little after noon, my mom prepared to drive Web to the sawmill. He worked the swing shift.

"I'll decide when I come home from work, if we should risk the six-hour drive to grandpa and grandma Granatelli's," he told us kids.

If the flooding hadn't worsened by the time Web arrived home around 10:30 p.m. he might - "might," he emphasized - be willing to make the long dark drive to grandpa and grandmas so the McKenna family would arrive there early the next morning.

"You kids better pack your suitcases and be ready to go," mom told us. "If daddy comes home and says he is willing to risk the trip, we could be driving to Oregon at a moments' notice."

We started packing around three p.m. while our mother finished ironing a stack of dress shirts for one of her housecleaning customers.

All afternoon, while the rain outside continued its downpour, us kids argued about what clothing we should take with us, what toys the younger kids should bring along and how much stuff we would have to leave behind so we could cram all of our Christmas presents, the baby's playpen, snow chains, emergency roadside kit and other necessities into the car, not to mention two adults and eight children.

As we packed, we kept our ears glued to the radio or the television and our eyes focused on the gloom outside. Shortly after dark the electricity went out and the lights flicked off and we were plunged into total darkness. The effect might not have been so devastating if the Christmas tree lights had somehow miraculously stayed on, but when the Christmas tree lights blinked off too the McKenna household mood turned from festive to worrisome.

"What if the lights don't come back on," I asked my mom.

"They'll come back on," she said.

"If we don't go to grandma and grandpa's can we open our presents tonight?" my sister Loretta asked.

Just like Loretta, I thought. She never wanted to wait for anything. Loretta looked just like our mom and was a year younger than me less four days. Four days every year she was the same age as me, which she loved and I hated. Loretta was a favorite of my aunts, another fact I resented. They always talked about how cute Loretta was, but I did not see her as being the least bit cute.

As far as I was concerned all Loretta did was throw "hizzy fits" (that's what my mom called her tantrums) when she didn't get her own way. I figured my aunts thought Loretta was cute because they were just girls sticking up for a girl. Still, I did actually love my sister. She and I were born of our mother's first marriage and the bond between us was forged of the knowledge that we were second-class citizens in a family where there were six newer half-sisters and brothers.

What made life especially difficult for me personally was the knowledge that Web did not consider me to be his real son.

I felt incredibly resentful about that.

Web often said before Michael and Georgie (my two half-brothers) were born, "I'd like a son of my own someday and I have no intention of giving up trying to have one until I succeed."

More than once, when I overheard Web making this statement, I choked back the urge to scream, "What am I, chopped liver?" I'd heard that term "chopped liver" somewhere before; most likely read it in one of the library books I regularly devoured. I didn't care much for liver and I figured most people felt the same, ergo, chopped liver was not a very good thing. Nor was I - at least in Web's eyes.

I tried to be a real son to Web. Before I came down with rheumatic fever, I hunted and fished with him and I loathed fishing. I played football and basketball and baseball in junior high school and thought I was athletic enough and tough enough that I could do well at sports in high school and make Web proud.

"Despite the name Francis, you are no weenie," Web acknowledged.

In fact, I insisted on my friends calling me Francis rather than Frank or Frankie, because I was determined to prove the point that this particular Francis didn't care two cents what kind of sissy image his name conjured up. I also had carried a B-plus average in my school studies, and worked odd jobs when I could find them during the summers.

Still, I knew Web did not consider me to be his real son. Too bad it took him so long to accomplish his goal of getting his own son, because I wound up with four more sisters (in addition to Loretta) before Web finally made good on his promise. Then, of course, he overdid it and produced not one son but two. Now there were eight kids in our family – five girls and three boys. Consequently, we were broke all the time, with barely enough food to go around, and I often found myself selfishly wishing I were an only child.

Half an hour after the electricity went off it came back on.

"Hooray!" we kids shouted.

"Good, now I can finish my ironing," my mom said.

Packing for the trip to Oregon resumed. Around six o'clock, mom announced she was finished with her ironing and needed to deliver it to the owner.

"I'll take Goldie and Ariane with me," she told me, indicating my eleven-year old and nine-year old sisters. "You stay here with Loretta and the rest of the kids."

Loretta and the rest of the kids. That meant I would be responsible for Loretta, eight-year old Grace, six-year old Margaret and the two boys, Michael and Georgie, who were three and two, respectively.

"I hope Georgie doesn't crap in his diapers while mom's gone," I thought to myself. "I'm not changing him if he does," I vowed.

As soon as mom drove off in the darkness to deliver her ironing Loretta began cajoling me to help her figure out what was in our Christmas packages.

"Don't you want to know what you're getting?" she asked peevishly.

"No! I don't," I said, attempting to explain to her for what I believed was the umpteenth time that I preferred being surprised.

"Oh, pooh!" Loretta said, flopping down on the floor in front of the Christmas tree and picking up a small, gaily wrapped present with her name on it.

"You never want to do anything I want to do," she said, shaking her package vigorously. It made a rattling sound inside and then there was a faint ding, like something had struck a small bell.

"Oh, I bet this is that charm bracelet I wanted," she exclaimed excitedly.

"It's probably a cat bell to put around your neck," I teased.

"Is not," Loretta retorted.

"Maybe it's just a box of old pennies."

"Why are you so contrary?" Loretta asked.

"I'm not contrary," I insisted. "I just don't want to know what my presents are before Christmas. If I knew, Christmas morning wouldn't be special. It'd just be another day."

"Well, I'd like to know," Loretta said. "Then I could savor the knowledge that I was getting what I wanted all the way up to Christmas."

"But what if it turned out you guessed wrong and you didn't get what you wanted?"

"Unggg! You make me so mad sometimes I could just swear," Loretta said. "But momma says we shouldn't swear, and anyway, I'm not going to do it in front of the little ones."

"Crap." I said.

"Francis! I'm going to tell momma!"

"You better not."

"Oh? Are you threatening me big man? I'm not afraid of you."

"Ah, what's the use of talking to you? You haven't got the brain God gave a goose."

"Have too. Quack. Quack. Quack."

"Geese don't quack, you know."

"Quack. Quack. Quack."

"Shut up!"

"Make me. Quack. Quack. Quack."

Realizing that this conversation was going nowhere, I stalked off to my room and slammed the door.

"You can't leave me alone out here." Loretta screamed at the closed door.

"Oh yeah!" I retorted. "That's what I'm doing."

Having my own room in a family of eight children was an absolute luxury. I understood that and appreciated it. I also appreciated the fact that Web, in spite of all his shortcomings, had actually stuck up for me when I asked to have my own room.

"He's a teenage boy," Web told my mom, "he needs his own space."

Being sick didn't hurt my cause either. I figured what the heck - take the breaks when you get 'em. The next house we rented, one with four bedrooms rather than three, I got my wish for my own room.

The girls all slept together in one room, which bugged Loretta to no end, the baby boys slept in another room, Web and my mom had their bedroom and I had mine. Mine wasn't much bigger than an oversized coat closet, but it was mine.

I worked out for a few minutes on the weight set in my room; two reps of arm curls for each arm, two reps of leg squats. The weight set had been a surprise present from my grandparents, to help me regain my strength.

As soon as my doctor gave me permission, I had started pumping iron. I still had a long way to go before my legs were as strong as they used to be, but my arms were shaping up pretty nicely.

Finally, I flopped down on my bed and tuned my transistor radio to a station in San Francisco. The radio had been an eighth-grade graduation present from my aunt Jeannie.

"You deserve a big surprise for graduating," Jeannie had told me.

I loved her for making me feel so special.

It amazed me that I could listen to music coming from San Francisco, three-hundred some odd miles from my home in the redwoods, on a little plastic doohickey that I could hold in one hand.

The Temptations hit *Smoke Gets in Your Eyes* came on. I thought back to my eighth-grade graduation dance when I'd spent most of the evening dancing with Candace Reulmann. Candy we called her at school.

"Cause she's sweet like candy," one of my classmates had drooled.

Candy and I hadn't paid much attention to each other previously, but we began making frequent eye contact in eighth-grade. I knew it didn't hurt that I'd played sports. Candy was a cheerleader, tall and blonde and graceful. She wore her hair in a pony tail most of the time, and I was a sucker for pony tails. She had big blue eyes and spoke in a voice that was somewhat shy and childish, yet at the same time very forthright and mature. I admired Candy because she spoke her mind to our teacher or in a crowd of our classmates even when she was obviously nervous.

But it wasn't until the night of graduation, during the sock hop in the gymnasium, that I actually spent any real time with Candy, actually held a real conservation with her and actually touched her. We danced to *Smoke Gets in Your Eyes*. She walked all the way across the gymnasium from where she'd been talking with other girls to ask me to dance.

"Would you do me the honor Francis?" she asked.

Do her the honor? I felt like I was the one being honored. My heart nearly leaped into my throat, my knees suddenly took to trembling and my palms got sweaty, but I managed to croak, "Okay."

I never held a girl who was physically attractive to me in my arms before. I'd hugged my sister - but only when I had to. I'd hugged my mother, my grandmother and my aunts, but that wasn't the same. Candy was not a relative or a family friend. She was, you know, a real girl – with a body, a body that possibly rivaled many of the ones I'd seen in Web's *Playboy* magazines.

Of course, I tried not to think of Candy the same way I thought of the women in *Playboy*. God probably wouldn't approve of that. No, it was safer, and I approved of myself more, if I thought of Candy as chaste and wholesome. As far as I knew she was.

Candy was so soft though, and she smelled fantastic. Her perfume was Desert Flower, she said. As she floated around the dance floor with me, I kept my right hand rigidly light on the small of her back, like she was precious china, and my sweaty left hand securely inserted into her palm.

I felt tingly and electrified by Candy's smile. Her lithe, responsive, physical presence moved in perfect rhythm and harmony with my own physical presence. I wanted to touch Candy more, but that thought probably was evil too. If I couldn't touch her more, I wished with all my heart that this moment would last forever.

But then *Smoke Gets in Your Eyes* ended and Candy suddenly melted away to the other side of the gym again. Some fast rock and roll came on, Elvis Presley, Chubby Checkers and the *Twist*, Bill Haley and *Rock Around the Clock*, Chuck Berry. I wanted to ask Candy to continue dancing with me, but I didn't know how to fast dance. I agonized about what to do.

Three more songs played. Then, blessed event! *Smoke Gets in Your Eyes* came on again.

I hurried across the dance floor before some other guy could beat me to Candy, like there was a hand pushing me from behind. About halfway across the floor, I noticed Greg Lupin headed her way too.

Greg was the quarterback of our football team. I thought I was going to miss my chance. But then, good grief! Candy was walking right past Greg, to me, putting her hands out to me, tugging me out onto the dance floor. I didn't even have to say anything!

Through the entire song, neither one of us said anything. But I felt us inching closer to each other, telegraphing our feelings to one another. My lungs tightened up until I wondered if I'd be able to keep on breathing. I hoped my palms weren't sweating too much. I felt an unfamiliar yet pleasant stirring in my soul. When the song ended, I nearly panicked. How was I going to keep Candy from leaving me again? I needn't have worried as it turned out.

"Do you want to get some punch?" she asked.

"Yeah," I wheezed appreciatively. "It's really warm in here."

"Yeah," she agreed.

We wandered over to the refreshment table. I noticed with extreme gratefulness that Candy had not let go of my hand. Of course she had to let go of it when I handed her a glass of punch. We stood with our punch for a minute, looking for a place to sit down.

"Would you like to sit down outside and catch some fresh air," I asked?

"That'd be great," she said.

We strolled outside, but just as we found a picnic table on the grass by the gym, where we could sit down, Carl Reinhardt, one of the tackles on the football team walked up to me and totally without warning, slugged me in the stomach as hard as he could! The air whistled out of me like I was a tire suddenly going flat.

I dropped my cup of punch. I held tight to my composure, in spite of my sudden discomfort, so as not to let Carl or Candy see my pain and looked at Carl as steely-eyed as I could.

I told him then through clenched teeth, with as much controlled anger as I could muster up, "Don't ever hit me again Carl, ever."

I wanted him to believe that I would kill him if he did. He appeared to buy it.

"It isn't right for you to steal Greg's girl," Carl muttered, but he stalked off and left me alone.

Greg happened to come along just then and apologized to me.

"I saw what happened, Francis," Greg said. "Carl's crazy. I sure hope you don't think I put him up to that. Sorry Candace."

"No harm done," I said through still-clenched teeth, keeping up the pretense that I was okay. "Just keep him away from me or he's going to get hurt."

"No problem," Greg said. "Hey, you going to play football in high school next year?"

"That's my plan," I said.

We didn't have much else to talk about. Candy suggested Greg bring me another glass of punch, which he actually did. Then Greg took his leave of us, looking envious of me, but not so envious that he wanted to slug me too.

When I finally regained my breath and composure Candy and I sat down at the picnic table and took up where we'd left off. As we talked, I recalled all the times I'd sat at that very table, eating lunch, talking with my friends. Next fall I was heading off to high school. Things would change. I wondered how much.

I looked at Candy and thought I would like to have a girlfriend like her in high school. Candy herself would be my first choice. I almost turned giddy with that idea. I'd never dared hope such a thing before. Having a girlfriend was infinitely better than wondering what might be wrapped up in a Christmas package, especially having a girlfriend like Candy. A girlfriend like Candy, versus a new shirt was no contest.

As if she were reading my mind, Candy asked me, "What are your hopes for high school, Francis?"

I didn't tell her I was hoping she would be my girlfriend.

"I'd like to make the varsity football and baseball squads my sophomore year and be voted All-County my junior and senior years," I said confidently. "Other than that I'm not sure. 'Course I'm hoping to get good grades so I can go to college."

"I want to go to college too," Candace sighed.

I began to imagine what it would be like to attend college with Candace.

After graduating maybe we'd get married and start careers. She'd be a famous model for a few years. Then, maybe we'd have a family. One thing for sure, I thought. We wouldn't have eight kids. No way! Two at the most. Then Candace blew my dream away like she had waved an evil magic wand in front of me.

"My only regret," she was saying, "is that I'm not going to be able to attend high school here. My dad got a job transfer and we're moving to Seattle next week."

"What?" I desperately wanted not to believe my ears.

"Next week!"

"I'm afraid so." We looked into each other's eyes longingly.

I suddenly was tempted to tell Candy I loved her. But I didn't know her well enough to tell her I loved her. Besides, my mom told me I couldn't even date until I was sixteen. That was still two years away. How could I love someone I couldn't even date? If Candace left I would never be able to date her. My night was ruined.

"Oh Francis," Candace said. "I wish I could stay here and go to high school with you. I really do. We could have so much fun together. But I guess it's not meant to be."

"I guess not," I mumbled bleakly, wondering why it wasn't meant to be, suddenly wanting not to look at her anymore. How could she do this to me? How could God do this to me? I felt totally betrayed.

"Francis, what are you thinking?" Candace asked.

"I - I - I hope everything works out for you," I lied. "Maybe we better go back inside now."

"Francis?"

"What?"

"I'm sorry!"

"Me too Candy. Me too," I groaned.

Candace set her punch cup down on the picnic table, reached out to me and took my free hand in her lap.

"Her hands are so beautiful!" I thought. "And I'll never hold them again."

Then Candace bent forward and softly kissed me on the cheek. I would never forget the warm caress of her breath on my face, the moist tenderness of her lips as they pressed against my skin. I could feel them even now.

Something stirred in me again. My heart suddenly felt tight. It probably wasn't good for my health to be thinking of Candace.

I leaped from my bed and bolted back out to the living room.

CHAPTER IV

"**A**re we finished packing yet," I demanded of Loretta.

"I think so," Loretta said, blinking at me like I had suddenly attacked her.

"Okay." I said. "Let's play a game with the little kids or something. I'm bored just lying around here waiting to find out if we're going to go to grandpa and grandmas."

Loretta and I tried to play Old Maid with Grace and Margaret but Margaret's attention span wasn't quite long enough for her to sit still through an entire game. Besides that, the two little boys kept interfering and demanding attention.

Finally, I organized a game of hide-and-go-seek. Everybody hid while I counted - a long count. Then I took my sweet time finding them. I found Loretta first. She never could hide very well. The two baby boys were next. They were too young not to give themselves away easily. Margaret came after that, then Grace.

It took a few minutes to locate Grace as she had stuffed herself into the laundry basket in the bathroom. I only found her when I poked my head into the bathroom a second time and heard muffled giggling. I lifted the lid of the laundry basket and there was Grace's curly hair sticking out from under the dirty laundry.

"I found Gracie," I yelled so the rest of the kids could hear. "I'm gonna' beat her back to base so she'll be it."

Grace scrambled from her hiding place, tipping the laundry basket over and strewing clothes behind her as she made a beeline for "base," which happened to be the living room couch. Her short little legs didn't carry her very fast so I pretended to stumble and fall as I was chasing her, thus allowing her to arrive back at base first.

"Fwee! She yelled, jumping on the couch with giddy triumph. "I'm fwee!"

"Yes you are," I agreed. "Now I'll have to be it again." I hung my head in mock defeat.

"I'll be it Fwancis," Grace offered.

She was a kind-hearted little thing. And she liked me a lot.

Whenever the family drove somewhere, Grace tried to sit next to me in the car. When we took a family walk Grace would always elect to hold my hand rather than someone else's.

"I'll be it again Punkin," I said. Punkin was my nickname for Grace because she was so round and chubby-legged. Besides, I figured with her personality she couldn't help but become a princess someday. I called her Punkin in memory of Cinderella because I saw her as a future Cinderella.

"You won fair and square Punkin," I told her. "Everybody hide again," I said.

We were into our fifth game of hide-and-go-seek, with me having been "it" twice, Loretta having been it twice and Grace - because she insisted - having been it once, when mom came home from delivering her ironing.

A cold blast of howling wind and rain followed her through the front door.

"The weather outside is . . ."

"Frightful!" Loretta offered.

"What?" our mom said, setting her purse down on the kitchen table and draping her wet coat over a chair to dry.

"Frightful," Loretta repeated.

"The weather outside is frightful," I explained. "You know, like the song?"

"I get it," mom laughed ruefully.

"You think we'll get to go to grandma and grandpa's?" Loretta inquired.

"I don't know honey," mom said. "We'll just have to wait until daddy gets home to see."

As it was only seven o'clock, "daddy" (which I never called Web) wasn't scheduled to arrive home for another three and a half hours. It was going to be a long wait as far as I was concerned.

Mom set about fixing some dinner for us. Before we sat down to eat, I turned the television to the local news channel. The news was not good. Most of the coverage that evening was devoted to the bad weather; exactly what us kids did not want to see. Mudslides were turning roads into gooey messes. Snow was blanketing the mountain passes. Flooding was rampant throughout the Pacific Northwest.

But so far, miracle of miracles! Highway 101, the route we would take much of the way to grandpa and grandma Granatelli's house in Cedar Grove remained open. And once we got past Grants Pass, we would turn onto U.S. 99 and leave most of the usual problem areas behind. We should have smooth sailing the rest of the way. We were all cheered by this wonderful piece of information.

We sat down to dinner and just about that time the electricity snapped off again.

Mom and I pulled candles out of the kitchen drawers while Loretta calmed the younger children. Once the candles were lit, we returned to the task of eating our dinner.

"We're having dinner by candlelight," Loretta observed, "how romantic."

"Fat lot you know about romance," I thought. I had never known Loretta to take any interest in boys other than to pester them.

"I wish the TV would come back on so we could finish watching the news," I said.

"Why don't you get your transistor radio out of your room and turn it on," mom suggested.

I retrieved my radio from my room and tuned it to a station giving the news.

It was then that we heard about the Umpqua River flooding. The Umpqua lay between us and grandpa and grandma's house. It crossed the highway in several places. The electricity came back on again a few minutes later.

After dinner we settled down to watch television: *What's My Line*, *The George Burns & Gracie Allen Show*, *The Bob Cummings Show* and whatever else was on that evening.

At nine o'clock mom put the little kids to bed: Michael and Georgie, Ariane, Grace and Margaret, dressing them in their warmest sleeping clothes so she could just bundle them up and put them on the mattress in the back of the station wagon should Web come home and announce we were, after all, making the drive north. Goldie, Loretta and I stayed up with mom, watching the weather outside, watching television, and waiting.

Nine thirty. Mom would be going after Web pretty soon.

Nine forty five.

Ten o'clock. Mom left to retrieve Web from work.

At ten fifteen I suggested turning the television off so we could hear the family station wagon when it pulled into the driveway.

Ten twenty.

Ten twenty five.

Ten thirty.

"They're here," Loretta shouted.

"Sh-h-h," I cautioned. "You'll wake the little ones."

Sure enough, the sound of the station wagon's engine grew loud in the driveway. We heard the squeak of brakes being applied, then the slamming of doors and tramping of feet coming toward the house. Loretta couldn't wait for the natural course of events any longer and ran to the front door jerking it open just as Web reached for the knob.

"Are we going to grandma and grandpas?" she asked, looking up into our stepfather's face.

"What's the weather report?" he asked, teasing her, making her wait for his answer.

"It's not bad," Loretta lied.

"Not bad huh? That's not what I heard."

Web and mom came on in the house and Web sat down and pulled off his boots.

Web was six feet tall, reed thin from smoking too many cigarettes, and hard muscled from working in the woods and in sawmills. His hands were rough and calloused from his years as a laborer. He had curly brown hair, brown eyes and full lips. He said he came from Kansas and was part Indian and part Irish.

He looked a lot like the Henry Fonda version of Tom Joad in *Grapes of Wrath*.

Web smelled, as he always did when he came home from work, like wet wood and pitch. I liked the smell of freshly cut wood, but wet sawmill logs had a peculiarly rancid odor that I didn't care for at all. I vowed again, as I had dozens of times before, that I would never, not ever, go to work in a saw mill.

"What's the weather report Francis?" Web asked.

He knew that I would give it to him straight. If there was one thing I did not do well it was lie. My face would always give me away. I had learned that hard fact about myself early on and that knowledge, along with the teaching I received in Sunday school made me virtually incapable of lying. Unfortunately, the rest of the family knew this as well as I did. I had this darned *good* streak in me that wouldn't go away. It was like I was cursed or something.

"There was a landslide on 101 near Orick but it sounds like they'll have it cleaned up by the time we get there," I reported. "And there's supposed to be some flooding of the Umpqua River around Roseburg."

"Are any roads closed that you know of," Web asked, looking not only at me, but also at mom, to make sure he was getting the straight poop.

"None that we've heard of," mom assured him.

"I don't know," Web said, slipping his suspenders off his shoulders. "We probably oughta' just stay home and make the best of it."

"No daddy!" Loretta protested.

I sensed that Web was prepared to make the drive north. He was just teasing Loretta, dragging out the suspense as long as he could. If he weren't willing to make the trip he would have said no right off. If he teased, you knew you had him. I was filled with joy. I loved going to my grandparent's house for Christmas.

"Tell you what," Web finally drawled. "I got to get out of these dirty clothes and take a shower then grab a little bite to eat. But if you all can be ready to go by the time I'm ready, well, I guess we'll go."

"Yay!" Loretta yelled.

"Yay!" I thought.

A flurry of busyness followed. First, all the luggage we were taking had to be stowed in the station wagon. Loretta and I were delegated this task. It didn't seem to matter if I was an invalid when there was work to be done. I had noticed this trend before and made a mental note of it now, so I could use the fact to my advantage next time I debated my mom about my fitness to resume normal activities.

Loretta and I donned our coats and made the obligatory trips to the car, getting good and wet in the process. Once the luggage, which really only consisted of a couple of battered old suitcases, was situated, the mattress our mom had made for the back of the station, was put in place.

Then all the Christmas presents - and there were plenty for a family of ten despite the economic situation of the McKennas - were placed around the periphery of the mattress. Then, after Loretta and I changed into dry clothes, it was time to start loading people.

"Does everybody have boots and mittens?" mom inquired of her brood.

"I've got mine momma," Loretta answered.

"I think we're all set," I replied.

"I need to sit up front so I don't get carsick," Loretta said.

"You never get carsick," I pointed out.

"I could," Loretta retorted.

"You do look kind of pukey," I laughed.

"Momma!" Loretta protested.

"Quiet, you too," mom commanded, "or daddy might be tempted to leave you here."

I knew that was an idle threat, but I didn't feel like taunting Loretta anymore anyway so I fell quiet. I really didn't mind if she sat in the front seat. I sure didn't want to. It would be too cramped in the front seat. I preferred sitting in the back seat with Grace and Goldie. Grace could have stretched out on the mattress with the other little kids, but she preferred sitting beside me. I did not want to disappoint her and I was not about to sit between my parents.

"Did you gas the car up today?" Web asked mom.

"All done," she replied. "I also had the oil checked and air put in the tires."

Mom bundled the babies up in blankets and we all trundled out to the car.

Once we were situated in our respective places, mom insisted that we say a little prayer before starting out. She was not a very religious person anymore, but she did still pray on special occasions.

"Lord," she intoned as we all bowed our heads, "Please watch over us and protect us as we travel to grandpa and grandma's house to celebrate your birth. We ask this in thy precious name, amen."

"Amen, we all repeated loudly.

With that Web started up the station wagon and we pulled out of the driveway. As we drove away from the house, I happened to look back. The house stood dark and forlorn now like all the life had suddenly been sucked out of it.

If the house had been a person it would look slump-shouldered, burdened down with overwhelming sadness and depression. It would have bent over under its heavy load of grief and wept bitterly. It would have moaned in the wind, crying for lost days of joy and happiness. I suddenly felt empty too, empathizing with the house. That was what death would be like I thought.

One day you were alive and warm, lit up with friends and family coming and going, then poof, someone threw a switch and you were dark and cold and your friends and family – your life - were all gone. I hated that thought. I knew I was being morbid, but I'd lain awake too many nights since my bout with rheumatic fever, contemplating death and afraid to die. I had been infinitely saddened by the idea that I would someday cease to exist. How could that be?

I had escaped death by blood poisoning and rheumatic fever, but what if we were involved in an accident on this trip and I died anyway, never to return home, never to play football, never to dance with a girl like Candy again? It was not a comforting thought that I would not be *here* anymore. Why did people have to die? I wondered briefly if I were having a premonition, but finally decided I was just being stupid.

Before we left the Fern Valley city limits Loretta was asking how long it would take to get to grandpa and grandma's house.

"It's going to take a long time," mom replied. "You might as well try to get some sleep. Everybody should try to get some sleep," she said, raising her voice so me and the other kids could hear.

"I'm not stopping except to get gas and to pee," Web informed us.

He wouldn't either, I reminded myself. He never did.

With Web, it was drive straight through as fast as possible, whether it took three hours or ten. He didn't like to stop. I had used the bathroom before we left the house, as all the kids had, but now I wondered if I could hold on until Web finally, reluctantly pulled into a gas station.

One thing was for sure. I was not going to go to sleep.

Even though it was dark out and I could see very little of the landscape rushing by, I was going to take in as much of it at sixty five miles per hour as humanly possible. I needed to make some kind of connection to the rest of the world if all I glimpsed of it in the dark were a few colored Christmas lights whizzing by.

I had felt disconnected way too long.

Chapter V

We reached Eureka, the official seat of Humboldt County, twenty five miles north of Fern Valley, just before midnight. There still was quite a bit of traffic and activity downtown, I noted. The next 93 miles of U.S. Highway 101, from Eureka to Crescent City, and the 100-plus miles across U.S. 199 between Crescent City and Grants Pass would be the toughest legs of the trip.

In daylight, and especially during the summer, the drive across U.S. 101 to Crescent City was beautiful. The narrow two-lane road followed the Pacific Ocean coastline, winding ribbon-like past the sparkling sandy beaches above Arcata and McKinleyville, past Trinidad Bay and Prairie Creek State Park and Big Lagoon, and through the redwoods.

The long arms of the giant skyscraping redwood trees filtered the sun, causing the few beams that did break through to look like heavenly shafts of gold. The effect created a chapel-like atmosphere.

"You can almost visualize God riding his royal chariot down those hazy tracks," my mom once said.

Countless painters had tried to capture the mysterious spirituality of the redwoods, with varying degrees of success. Photographers tried too. "But remember that one guy who got run over by a logging truck when he laid down on the road to shoot his picture?" Loretta said.

Different varieties of green ferns filled shady spaces between the redwood trees and native wild flowers and rhododendrons bloomed profusely along the roadside, creating a red, yellow, pink and white palette of color. Interspersed with all that were open stretches where you could see the blue-green waters of the Pacific Ocean crashing relentlessly against rocky seaweed-covered reefs far below.

But now Highway 101 was just dark, damp and dangerous.

The Red Jacket   Jim Perkins

The only items of any scenic value along this stretch of road in the dark would be the Trees of Mystery tourist attraction at Klamath, with its huge statue of Paul Bunyan, and Babe his big blue ox.

Paul Bunyan was a giant plastic or fiberglass figure standing about forty nine feet tall in front of the gift shop at the Trees of Mystery. I couldn't remember if the Trees of Mystery Paul Bunyan matched the description of the mythical Paul Bunyan I'd read about in elementary school, but this Paul Bunyan was black haired, sported a thick black beard and wore a red flannel shirt, blue pants with suspenders to hold them up and ten foot-high black boots. In his right hand he carried a twenty four foot-long double-edged ax. His ox Babe, stood as tall as him and sported horns that spread out at least 20 feet.

One time not too long after we moved to the redwoods, Web and mom had taken us to see the Trees of Mystery. When Loretta walked up to Paul Bunyan, his voice boomed out over a loudspeaker and said, "Hi there!" Loretta about jumped out of her skin and wet her pants. I thought that was pretty funny.

A herd of Roosevelt Elk populated the same general area as the Trees of Mystery. They were beautiful animals. The bucks sported majestic racks of horns and mantles of fur around their necks that reminded me of plush v-necked cardigan sweaters or mink stoles. The elk would often stand right out on the highway and defy motorists to drive around them.

Occasionally, an elk lost this game of chicken and died as a result. Of course they usually made quite a mess of the cars that struck them too. A few years earlier, my mom had been driving this stretch of road on a return trip from Oregon and had hit an elk that suddenly jumped out in front of her. Fortunately, the only damage to our car was a crumpled fender. Web and I got quite a scare, however, when we climbed out of the car to drag the elk off the highway and it jumped up and ran off just as we reached down to grab hold of its hind legs!

"Holy Christ," Web had screeched.

49

The stretch of U.S. 199 from Crescent City to Grants Pass wasn't all that beautiful any time of the year as far as I was concerned. I decided if I just had to give in to sleep during the trip that would be the area where I could allow myself to nod off and not feel guilty. But I was determined not to go to sleep at any point of the trip.

About 10 miles out of Eureka, just past the college town of Arcata, a car full of people passed Web, accelerating around him on a curve, crossing the double-yellow line with another vehicle coming the other way.

"What the hey!" Web exploded. "People drive like danged fools!"

I noted a Humboldt State College sticker in the back window of the vehicle that passed us. College kids probably, on their way home to Crescent City. I wished them a safe trip.

"I hope you don't drive like that when you get your license," Web said, looking at me darkly in the rear view mirror.

"I won't," I promised, meeting Web's ominous gaze.

"Francis, will you take me for a ride when you get your license?" Grace asked, squeezing my hand.

"Sure Punkin," I told her. "You'll be my first passenger."

Grace beamed up at me, sighed happily and snuggled her head against my rib cage.

"He'll probably get a ticket for speeding," Loretta predicted loudly from the front seat.

"Francis will be careful," mom assured everyone. "If he gets a ticket, he'll lose his insurance."

"Not to mention his driving privileges," Web warned.

"He has to take driver's ed before he can get his license," mom said. "And he might not be able to get into driver's ed right away. He might have to wait until his junior year of school because he's been sick and has missed so much. There might be a lot of other kids ahead of him."

"Wait?" I thought. Gees I hope I didn't have to wait too long. I knew my mother would like it if I never drove. But there was a good chance I *would* have to wait until my junior year of high school to take driver's education training. Not starting school until the second half of my sophomore year (if my mother even let me do that) would probably put me way at the end of the waiting line. Other guys my age would be driving long before me. Of course, I had heard that driver's training selection depended somewhat on having good grades too and on one's maturity level.

I had good grades, and as the oldest of eight children, I bet I was way more responsible than most of my peers. I *could* get picked for driver's training right away rather than having to wait until I was a junior.

I wondered what Candy would think if she could see me driving a car. It seemed kind of weird that I was on my way to Oregon and Candy was only one more state away. If only I could drive the extra miles from Cedar Grove to Seattle to see her while we were on Christmas vacation. Too bad I'd have to drive my parent's station wagon to do that though. Girls were more impressed with a guy who had his own car.

Unfortunately, there was no way I could afford my own car; at least not for awhile. I'd have to secure some pretty good employment next summer to be able to afford a car. My mom probably would expect me to contribute a hefty portion of my earnings to helping the family too. Then, after buying my own school clothes, which I knew she would also expect, there wouldn't be much money left over for transportation.

I became so engrossed in daydreaming about my driver's license and what kind of car I might be able to afford, I forgot to watch for Paul Bunyan and Babe, and any elk feeding along the road. If there were any elk I didn't notice. We reached Crescent City and breezed right through it.

It was still raining when we reached Crescent City, but it always seemed to rain in that town anyway, since it was right next to the ocean. The sound of the rain falling on the car made me wish I could go to the bathroom, but obviously, I was going to have to hold on. Web was determined to "make good time," as he put it, and he was doing so.

I noted that all the little kids appeared to be wide awake. I could hear Michael and Georgie playing and giggling in the back, with Margaret tickling and teasing them. Ariane and Grace were playing with their dolls in the seat beside me and Loretta was chattering nonstop about the scenery, to our parents in the front seat. Everyone sounded fairly content, I noted. It was a rare occasion in my family when everyone was contented at the same time.

Just north of the California/Oregon border we were stopped for about twenty minutes while an Oregon Department of Transportation highway crew cleaned up the remains of a small mudslide partially blocking the northbound lane of U.S. 101. This was an opportunity for mom to inquire after the little ones in the far back of the station wagon.

"I don't smell any poopy diapers yet," Ariane reported. Everyone giggled at this bit of good news.

"I'm hungry," Grace said.

"Me too," Margaret piped up.

"Francis hand that bag of food up here," mom directed me, meaning the large grocery bag full of treats she had packed for the trip.

I did as I was told and mom popped the lid off a large Tupperware container and asked, "Who wants a cookie?"

Choruses of "I do, I do," were met with chocolate chip and oatmeal raisin cookies being passed around. Mom poured coffee from a Thermos bottle into a plastic cup and handed it and a couple of chocolate chip cookies to Web.

"Francis, there's punch in that insulated gallon jug if you'll pour some for the little kids," mom said.

The gallon jug was on the floor between my feet. I poured punch into paper cups and passed the cups around making sure nobody spilled the sticky, cherry-flavored liquid in the car. Finally, when everyone's thirst was slaked, I poured myself some punch and drank it. Then I really needed to go to the bathroom. Fortunately, Web finished his coffee and cookies and reported that he was going to step outside for a minute to smoke a cigarette.

"Can I go outside with you?" I asked urgently.

Understanding my problem Web said yes, "Just make sure you find a big enough tree to hide behind," he laughed.

Despite the chilling wind and rain, I found a big redwood and relieved myself with a grateful sigh. Finally, the road crew waved us on.

Web muttered briefly that the "good time" we had been making had been lost, but maybe with a little bit of luck, we could get it back. That meant driving in excess of the speed limit, something Web rarely did, but the car surged forward as he stomped his foot on the gas pedal and for the next several miles, I noted that he kept a wary eye on his rear view mirror for any suspicious looking cars coming up behind him.

We reached Grants Pass around four o'clock in the morning. It was still dark outside. All of the other kids had fallen asleep. But Web had to stop in Grants Pass to gas the car up and several of them woke up. As Web gassed the car up, mom changed Michael and Georgie's diapers.

"Francis, you and Loretta take the girls to the restrooms," mom directed us.

Loretta and I did as we were told and deposited the girls back in the car. Then I went to use the men's restroom.

I finished "doing my duty" and used what opportunity I had until Web yelled "all aboard," to poke around the gas station a little bit and to reconnoiter the surrounding landscape.

The city of Grants Pass was already starting to wake up. Empty logging trucks drove by at frequent intervals. A few townies and some weary travelers were pulling into a nearby 24-hour cafe for an early breakfast.

"I wish our family could stop at a restaurant to eat breakfast," I thought longingly.

But I knew that would be prohibitively expensive to go out to breakfast with eight children. I promised myself that someday, someday when I was an adult on my own, traveling to some unknown destination, that I would stop for breakfast at a restaurant. I would order orange juice, eggs and sausage, and hash browns, maybe even pancakes, and I'd flirt with a pretty waitress.

The Grants Pass city park was across the street from the gas station.

"I also wish I could visit that park," I thought.

All the times that my family had driven through Grants Pass, we had never stopped and visited the park. The park had tall trees, tennis courts and baseball fields. In the dark it looked like a real nice place. A river, which I could just make out and later learned was the Rogue River, ran along the north boundary of the park. I noticed that the river was swollen with rain, running right up to the top of its banks and lapping hungrily at the park lawn.

A large white sign with blue lettering, nailed to a tree just out of reach of the water and illuminated by a bare, naked light bulb said, "Jet Boat Rides. Scenic jet boat rides on the Rogue River." A jet boat ride on the Rogue River sounded like a lot of fun.

"Someday," I promised myself, "I'll come back to Grants Pass and take a jet boat ride too."

I imagined riding a jet boat through the canyons of the Rogue would be like riding a horse through a canyon in a Zane Grey novel. The boat would take me between narrow cliffs where moss and ferns hung down from the clay banks and there would be big pools of deep green water with twenty-pound salmon swimming lazily around in them.

Web called out for everybody to get back into the car.

"We're leaving in two minutes," he said heading for the bathroom to relieve himself. "Anybody not in the car when I come out of the bathroom is going to get left behind."

We scurried to resume our places in the station wagon. Ariane asked mom if she could sit in the front seat for awhile. This request did not go over well with Loretta, and I would just as soon she had remained in the front seat, but mom acquiesced to Ariane, and Loretta joined Grace and me in the back seat.

Loretta and I made sure we kept Grace between us - which was more than okay with Grace - partly because we each wanted to sit by a window, but just as importantly, because we did not want to have to sit right next to each other.

Within seconds, Web returned from the men's room and the trip resumed with mom taking her turn at driving. It wasn't long before almost everyone in the car had fallen back to sleep. It got real quiet in the car except for Web's sonorous snoring.

The next few miles were uneventful. We were headed north on U.S. Highway 99 toward Roseburg. Once we reached Roseburg, it would only take a couple more hours to arrive in Cedar Grove.

CHAPTER VI

S uddenly, I was jolted by the blast of a trucker's air horn, the screech of brakes and my mom screaming hysterically.

I quickly tried to gather my wits, but all I could see was a silvery screen of raindrops pelting our windshield and the gleaming chrome radiator of a Peterbilt eighteen-wheeler looming directly in front of our station wagon. My mom was frantically cranking the steering wheel of our car to avoid a head-on collision.

Web jerked wide awake and yelled "Holy Christ!"

I know I will never forget the blood curdling scream that tore from my own throat and the look of guilty terror that I saw on the truck driver's face as the 18-wheeler jackknifed past us and somehow managed to miss us.

Our station wagon did a complete three hundred and sixty degree turn - several times if I remember correctly - and wound up headed southbound on the other side of the highway before mom could bring it to a stop. When the car finally stopped I could feel the rear wheels trying to dig into the muddy shoulder of the road and I prayed with all my strength that the car would not roll over the embankment and kill us all anyway, now that we had miraculously escaped being annihilated by the truck.

No sooner had mom brought the station wagon to a halt than the truck driver leaped from the cab of his vehicle and ran back to us to see if we were alright. As he jerked open the door of our station wagon, I noticed that his belly hung over blue jeans held up by a silver-buckled cowboy belt, and that he was wearing a coffee and snuff-stained tee shirt, an unbuttoned red-checkered wool shirt and leather slippers. His eyes were wild with fear and I think his scraggly grey hair, which was tied back in a pony tail, would have stood on end if it could have.

He might have looked like Santa Claus, except for the snuff stains and ponytail. At least, I had never envisioned Santa Claus as a user of snuff.

"My God Lady!" the truck driver croaked, "I thought you people were goners."

"We're alright," mom assured him with a frightened whisper.

"What happened?" Web demanded crossly, shaking his head to clear the cobwebs.

"It's my fault," mom told Web, putting a reassuring hand on his leg. "I must have fallen asleep."

"I never been so scared in my life," the truck driver said.

I believed the truck driver meant what he said, because his hands shook violently and he suddenly leaned against the station wagon for support. Then he did what I considered a curious thing for a tough, road-hardened truck driver. He bent over and threw up all over his slippers.

"Eww!" Loretta exclaimed.

"Eww!" Grace echoed.

The girl's exclamations of disgust broke the tension and everyone laughed hysterically.

But no sooner had we started laughing than mom burst into tears. "I almost killed my family," she sobbed. "I'll never drive again."

"We're okay honey," Web assured her.

He put his arms around her and let her sob into his shoulder for a few minutes, then lifted her head, looked her straight in the eyes and said, "You have to continue driving for a little while."

"You can't let this get to you. It happens to almost everybody sometime in their life."

"He's right lady," the truck driver said, wiping the remains of vomit from his lips with a soiled white pocket hanky. "You don't get back behind the wheel immediately after something like this happens, you might never be able to."

"But, but . . ." mom protested.

"You gotta' do it babe," Web reiterated. "You gotta' do it."

"Look folks, if you're all okay, I need to get going," the truck driver said. "I'm late as it is, though I think I'm going to be driving a lot slower the rest of the way. You think you're going to be okay?"

"We're okay," Web assured him. "Thank you for stopping."

"The least I could do," the truck driver said. As he squished back toward his truck in his now slimy slippers he said, "Merry Christmas."

"Merry Christmas," Grace called from the back seat in her sweet little voice.

"Merry Christmas," we all chorused.

Hopefully, it would be a merry Christmas, I thought. We had narrowly escaped death. What else could happen? I was full enough of Christmas good cheer that I quickly dismissed the old superstition about bad things happening in threes.

Web convinced mom to pull the station wagon back onto the road to continue driving. She was nervous and Web and I both kept reassuring her that she would be alright. After twenty miles or so she started to relax again.

"I'll never ever fall asleep at the wheel again," she promised Web.

"Don't worry about it," Web said gruffly. "Everything turned out all right."

After a few more minutes of driving mom turned to Web and said, "I'd like for you to drive now. I have a headache and I'd really like to close my eyes and get some rest."

"Okay," Web said. "Pull over and I'll drive. I could use a cigarette break anyway."

Mom pulled off the road. After hastily smoking an Old Gold filter-tipped cigarette, Web slid behind the wheel of the station wagon.

"I wish it would stop raining," he said peevishly as he drove back onto the highway. "We might have to stop and put water wings on this dang car." As it turned out, Web was right to worry. The nearer we got to Roseburg, the higher the Umpqua River rose.

The river roughly paralleled the highway and in the beams of the station wagon lights, Web and I, the only people in the car who stayed awake, could see the dark brown water chewing hungrily at the shoulders of the road. We also could see ample evidence of the havoc the flooding river was wreaking in the flat farmland alongside the road. Water surrounded farm houses and barns. Cattle and other livestock, seeking the highest ground they could find had congregated on dry little hummocks when they could reach them. The poor things looked like stranded travelers, I thought. I wondered again if the animals would be as terrified as I would be in their situation. I remembered the newspaper story I read and decided the cows would certainly be frightened.

The idea of drowning, gasping for air as a whirling eddy of muddy gritty brown water poured into my mouth and throat, then sucked me under and dragged me miles from home before my body was deposited lifeless in some unsuspecting person's front yard, did not at all appeal to me.

I still did not understand why people had to die, especially good people. I also realized I wasn't acting especially good lately.

Besides the farm buildings and animals surrounded by water, there was debris piled all along the edge of the road at the high mark of the river; logs, a wash machine, a baby's stroller . . . these were a few of the things I could see as we drove along. I wondered how much more debris had already been washed away by the flood waters.

Suddenly, there was a detour sign! Our car was on top of the sign before Web could react. The car smacked into the sign and the sign exploded into large splinters of wood that hit our windshield with a "Whack." Web jammed on the brakes and the car came to a stop just inches from the raging flood waters. Right in front of our bumper, now clearly visible in the car's headlights, the angry swollen Umpqua frothed past us.

"Holy Christ!" Web exclaimed for the second time that morning. "We just about plunged off into the drink."

Mom was startled awake by Web's shouted expletive. She rose up from her slumber to see what the problem was and shrieked when she saw the flood waters only inches away.

"Web, what happened?" she cried.

"Some yahoo put a detour sign up, Web exclaimed, "but they put it too close to the river. By the time I saw the sign it was almost too late to stop."

"That was way too close," he added with a shudder.

"I'll go along with that," I said. "Holy Christ!"

"Francis!" my mom exclaimed.

"Sorry. I said. "I just can't believe how close we came to driving into the river."

We had just experienced our second brush with death on this trip.

I was starting to take that saying about bad things happening in threes far more seriously.

I suddenly had a vision of our fifty-seven Chevrolet station wagon bobbing down the Umpqua, the McKenna family inside, screaming for help and people along the shore of the river pointing at us and saying, "Hey. Look at that blue station wagon floating down the river. It looks like there's people are in there. You think they need help?"

"I feel sick," Loretta said. She too had been awakened by Web's shouted expletive.

"Well, step outside and throw up," Web told her.

"No!" she protested. "The river might get me."

"We should be so lucky," I thought.

"Well," I gotta' smoke a cigarette," Web said. "If you wanna' step outside for a breath of air, I'll be right here to watch out for you."

Loretta declined Web's offer, deciding that she didn't feel all that sick after all. In fact, nobody dared to get out of the car. The river was just too close and too menacing. Strangely enough, the youngest kids had remained asleep in spite of the commotion.

But Web clearly needed a cigarette. He exited the station wagon, lit up an Old Gold and walked around in front of the car to look more closely at the roiling river. He stood there in the rain smoking his cigarette, brooding over the terrible fate that almost befell him and our family. I thought he looked like he was sizing the river up, sort of like an angry boxer preparing to fight a tough opponent.

It was like Web was thinking, "You almost got me, but you didn't. Now you'll wish you had. Next time I'll be ready for you and you are going to be the one who gets the surprise."

I had seen Web's look before and I didn't like it.

Once when Web had drunk too much beer at a picnic, he'd picked an argument with another guy and the other guy sucker punched Web in the stomach. Web just totally lost control of himself then and would have stomped the guy into the ground if mom hadn't grabbed him in a bear hug, pinning his arms to his sides.

"Let me go Mary Catherine," Web had hissed maniacally. But mom would not let him go until the other guy left.

I didn't like the idea of having to defy Web. The one time I did was more than enough. I knew I would probably wind up getting hurt very badly next time around. I might be big enough physically to fight Web if I had to, but I wasn't sure I was mentally or emotionally tough enough. Web's psychological makeup made him too darned dangerous.

Web smoked two cigarettes, while brooding at the river then finally climbed back into the car.

"We shouldn't have come on this trip," mom said. "I'm sorry Web."

"Whadya' talkin' about," Web responded harshly. "We're almost there now. "Couple more hours and we'll be at your folks and we'll forget all about this."

"I hope so," mom said.

"We're gonna' be fine," Web growled. "Providing we don't get hit by a bolt of lightning or buried by an avalanche or something."

Web backed the station wagon away from the river's edge and looked around for the road that was supposed to detour us away from the flood waters. He found a farm road forking off the east side of the highway that looked dry, and drove cautiously along it for five or six miles until it came back to U.S. 99.

"I hope it's safe to get back on the highway now," he said. I don't think I want any more surprises this trip."

Fortunately, there were no more surprises. At seven o'clock we reached the outskirts of Cedar Grove. I started looking for the familiar landmarks that told me we were getting closer to my grandpa and grandma's home. First came Aunt Ramona's house. Aunt Ramona was actually my grandma's aunt. Aunt Ramona was very old and her house, a Victorian-style structure with lots of "gingerbread" trim, was dilapidated and in a sad state of disrepair. It badly needed some serious yard care and a coat of paint.

The inside of the house was even worse. I wrinkled my nose remembering the way the house smelled inside. It reeked of stale body odor, grease, hot onions and mold. Aunt Ramona was very fat and wore dirty old muumuu dresses and fuzzy slippers with all the fuzz worn off, run over at the sides and so loose she had difficulty keeping them on her feet. Her hair was white and sparse and stringy. She was almost an exact opposite of my grandma who was tall and lean and always kept herself neat and orderly.

Aunt Ramona's house was always dark inside, with all the shades drawn to keep the sun out. There were slip covers on the furniture in the living room, but the slip covers were so dirty I couldn't even imagine what the sofa and chairs underneath looked like. Dirty dishes always littered the kitchen counters. Leftover food usually littered the dining table. I don't think Aunt Ramona ever opened a window. I was pretty sure she hadn't cleaned her house in a long, long time. Of course she wasn't really able to do much, and her husband Uncle Ray wasn't much help either.

Uncle Ray was a grizzled old coot who sat around chewing tobacco and spitting juice into an empty two-pound coffee can. Sometimes he didn't spit cleanly and tobacco juice ran down his beard and dribbled onto his soiled undershirt. He wore the kind of undershirt that had no sleeves and his hairy armpits showed when he raised his arms to do anything.

Unfortunately, my mom and grandma always felt obligated to take all us kids to see Aunt Ramona and Uncle Ray whenever we came to Cedar Grove. I knew sometime during the holidays we were going to wind up visiting there.

Next, came the Frosty Freezer drive-in restaurant. I liked the Frosty Freezer. My grandpa often took me to the Frosty Freezer for ice cream, or even better, a cheeseburger, onion rings *and* ice cream. My grandpa usually took me to Frosty Freezer when he wanted to escape the house and get out of some chore grandma had lined up for him. These were special occasions for me, occasions when I didn't have to share grandpa with anyone else.

Grandpa Granatelli was as guileless and straightforward as a man could be. What you saw in grandpa Granatelli was what you got. He never harbored a mean thought about other people that I knew of. He liked everybody and always managed to find good in others.

I always thought if I did become a priest – which I was determined not to do - it would be because of my grandpa. He was this strapping big Italian guy who stood six feet tall and weighed one-hundred ninety pounds, had dark curly hair and loved to polka, drink wine and laugh. Yet he was more deeply spiritual than any other man I'd ever known. He never missed confession, for instance, and it always impressed me that someone who obviously enjoyed life so much would readily confess his sins and actually seemed to enjoy the experience.

"Why not?" he once asked me. "Confession cleanses the soul. I'm a new man afterward. That seems like a pretty good deal to me."

So many Roman Catholics I knew seemed to feel that confession and other practices of the church were meaningless duties, to be practiced only because they had to, because they feared eternal damnation, not because they really believed. But my grandpa embraced the practices of the church as beneficial, subsequently, I don't think he suffered much from guilt – unlike my grandma, who also faithfully confessed her sins, but didn't seem to come away from the experience feeling cleansed.

I considered myself a younger replica of my grandpa, the only difference being that I didn't yet drink wine and hadn't yet learned to appreciate dancing.

Grandpa's eyes were deep blue and twinkled like finely cut sapphires when he laughed and he liked to laugh. I was the same way; at least I had been, before I caught rheumatic fever. Women loved grandpa for his good looks and good-natured bonhomie, although in recent years, my grandma was not always among his admirers.

I think what my grandma objected to most was all the attention grandpa got when he had a little wine in him and he launched into one of his tall tales. Other people really liked grandpa's stories, but grandma seemed pretty bored by them. I personally could sit and listen to my grandpa talk about the old days in Italy and about his early experiences in America for hours.

Grandpa Granatelli was one of more than twelve million immigrants who passed through the portals of Ellis Island in New York City, seeking a better life in America, during the peak years of 1892 to 1924. Grandpa had grown up on a small farm outside the northern Italian city of Bolzano.

I looked Bolzano up in an encyclopedia. During its early days the city was ringed by ancient castles and it was a gateway to the Dolomites, a famous rock-climbing area of the Italian Alps. Bolzano was an ancient trading town once ruled by the Tyrolean archduchess Claudia de Medici.

Unlike many of his fellow immigrants, grandpa discerned right away that New York City was not the place he wanted to stay. He was not looking for Italy in America. He wanted the freedom to be American in more wide open spaces. He made his way out West, to Oregon, and found work in heavy construction, spending many years helping build a dam just outside Cedar Grove.

One of the stories my grandpa often told was the one about his father taking him into Bolzano to sell the family's fruits and vegetables. After successfully hawking their produce, grandpa and his father ate lunch at a little café by a lake and his father bought him a beer.

Grandpa said he was twelve years old at the time and it was a very special occasion because his father was finally acknowledging him as a man.

"Six years later I was sent to America so I could have a better life," grandpa said.

He never saw his father again.

I envied grandpa for what little time he had with his father though. At least he'd had enough time with his father that he could still remember him. I had no recollection of my father whatsoever.

After the Frosty Freezer came the railroad station. Once we reached the railroad station we would turn right, or east, and proceed along Cedar Grove Avenue past the city park then turn south one block. Another block and we would turn left onto Lincoln Street and there would be grandpa and grandma's house, sitting atop a rise, overlooking the town of Cedar Grove.

The railroad station, painted a dirty yellow-gold color was quiet this time of morning. The three sets of tracks and the switches in front of the station set empty. I vaguely remembered boarding a train at this station once when I was very young. But I couldn't remember where I had gone.

I only remembered the gentle swaying of the passenger car as we rolled along through the countryside and that the trip had been exciting, with vistas of the big wide world whizzing passing me until I was almost dizzy. I longed to explore the world and see what was beyond the windows.

Then I came down with rheumatic fever and I was even more confined.

Across the street from the railroad station, at the northwest corner of the intersection was a Ford dealership.

The dealership had been there as long as I could remember. Grandpa and grandma had bought their '49 Ford there. I could just discern what looked like a new Ford Fairlane convertible in the showroom of the dealership.

This intersection was the east end of downtown Cedar Grove. If you proceeded west you entered the heart of the town with its barbershops, hardware stores, department stores, florist shops, city hall, banks and so on. On the southwest corner of the intersection stood the Hotel Cedar Grove, a once-respectable establishment, but now a seedy, rundown, rooming house where space was rented by the month rather than the night. The hotel still housed the Greyhound Bus depot. I remembered that there used to be a barbershop and shoeshine stand inside the hotel too.

Grandpa took me to the barbershop for a haircut once and afterward we both had our shoes shined. I cherished that memory. That was one of the times in my life that I'd really felt special. The shoeshine man was an older black man who seemed gentle and content with his work. I remember he smiled at me a lot as he shined my shoes and he softly whistled a song that I recognized as a gospel hymn, though I didn't know its title.

Right or wrong, I felt like that shoeshine man was giving me extra special service. I was intrigued that he didn't just use polish straight out of a can on my shoes. He mixed the polish with something else – sort of a watery mixture – probably spit, grandpa said - and the resulting shine was marvelous.

"I can see my face in the toes of my shoes!" I exclaimed to Grandpa. What a luxury to have someone else, besides myself, shine my shoes; especially when the man really knew what he was doing.

Finally, we turned up Cedar Grove Avenue then passed the city park.

I had spent many a happy afternoon at the city park, playing on the swings, climbing on the monkey bars, running around playing tag under the huge oak trees with my aunt Jeannie who was only five years older than me and my aunt Giselda (Gizzy, or Dizzy Gizzy if we really wanted to get her goat) who was only seven years my senior.

I'd even tried my hand at tennis once or twice but hadn't been able to hit the ball hard enough to give my aunts a real game. I thought I could give them a game now.

The other cool thing about the park was that it was only a few steps away from my grandparent's house. It was so close that my mom would let me go play there by myself even when I was little.

In the summer, blackberry bushes grew over the ditches alongside the road to the park and I liked to help my grandma pick the blackberries so she could make jelly and blackberry cobbler.

You had to be careful when picking blackberries not to grab one of the green beetles on the vines. Those were called stinkbugs and for good reason. Of course it was almost inevitable that you're arms were going to get scratched up from doing battle with the thorny vines.

But oh, the sweet smell of blackberries heated up by the warm summer sun and the sweeter taste of blackberry cobbler hot from the oven. Too bad Aunt Ramona's home didn't smell more like blackberries and less like sweat and mold.

Chapter VII

And then we had arrived!

Grandpa and grandma's house sat on a low rise overlooking Cedar Grove and it was bathed in the morning light like my personal shrine. I drank the sight in and savored it. I didn't know how many more years my grandparent's would be alive. When they died, I might not ever come here again and this place was more of a home to me than anywhere else. I wanted to remember it better than I remembered the Frosty Freeze or the railroad station or the Cedar Grove Hotel; way better.

I had lived here with my grandparents several months while my mom fought for her divorce from my dad. After mom married Web, we never lived anyplace more than a couple of years. My grandparents' house was my anchor. When we came here, I felt safe and secure.

The house stood two stories tall. A covered porch skirted the front. A dormer window looked over the porch. The dormer let light into my aunt Gizzy's bedroom. The grassy front yard flowed downhill from the front porch to the detached single-car garage where my grandpa and grandma's '49 Ford was sheltered. An iron gate with an arch over it, opened off the gravel driveway onto the cement walk that led to the house's front door. A climbing rose bush, its pink blooms now gone, laced its way over the arch above the gate. Other rose bushes lined the fence along the perimeter of the yard.

The fence was as sturdy as a man could build it. My grandpa had used sawed-off telephone poles for posts and attached heavy-gauge steel stock fencing to the poles. One neighbor had remarked that it appeared old man Granatelli was building a fence strong enough to keep elephants out.

"No, grandpa had retorted, "just strong enough to keep the grandkids in."

Grandpas' two prized holly trees stood between the fence and the front of the house. They reached at least ten feet tall and were loaded with the red berries that were so symbolic of the season. Grandma took cuttings from the holly trees each Christmas season and decorated the house liberally with them. A filbert tree stood in back of the garage. Blue Jays loved the filbert tree. But Grandpa didn't like the Blue Jays.

"Thieving buggers," he called them. He often shot at the thieving buggers with a pellet gun he kept propped up against a wall where a double-sash window looked out into the yard.

I knew when I walked into my grandpa and grandma's parlor that there would be a rack of filberts spread out on a wire rack hanging from the ceiling of the room, drying. We would eat a lot of filberts in the next few days, cracking their hard little shells between the steel jaws of a carved silver nutcracker, then flicking the shells into the living room fireplace to burn. Grandma always had a big bowl of nuts set out. Besides the filberts, she included pecans, walnuts, almonds, Brazil nuts and peanuts.

Grandpa's cherry tree and a couple of apple trees stood in the backyard. Grandpa had grafted a few different varieties of cherries onto the cherry tree and several different varieties of apples onto his apple trees. He bragged about his grafting prowess to anybody who would listen. A garden plot lay between the apple trees. A smokehouse and woodshed were located in the southeast corner of the yard.

I had split a lot of kindling in the woodshed. But my favorite place on my grandpa and grandma's property was the acre of pasture on the west side of the house; more specifically, its small two-story red barn.

The barn housed chickens, a milk cow and grandpa's big barrels of homemade wine. I enjoyed gathering eggs in a basket my grandmother would send with me to the barn. I marveled at how warm the eggs felt in their beds of straw even when the hens weren't sitting on them. I thought the gentle clucking of the hens was soothing.

The cow's name was Bess. She was a beautiful Swiss brown. Grandpa milked her by hand and I liked to watch him. Grandpa would sling a rope around Bess' rump to keep her from kicking then he would draw his three-legged milking stool up to her side.

"Easy now Bess," grandpa would say, "I'm just here to take a little milk for the children."

Bess would then swish her tail in grandpa's face and grandpa would yelp.

"Goldang it Bess!"

Once Bess and grandpa sorted out who was boss, grandpa would reach under her, grab a teat and gently start pulling on it. Warm white milk would froth up in the galvanized pail while Bess munched greedily on the hay grandpa had forked into her manger. Each of Bess's teats gave up its quota of milk until the pail became full.

The milking done, grandpa would scrape any manure Bess had dropped onto the concrete floor into a drainage ditch, and then chase it with a strong stream of water from a nearby hose out into the barnyard. The milk would later be poured from the pail into glass pitchers and deposited in the kitchen refrigerator. During the night thick layers of cream would rise to the top of the pitchers. In the morning I would eat cold cereal or hot oatmeal with large dollops of cream on top (and rich brown sugar if I ate oatmeal). Nothing could ever be better!

But before grandpa and I returned to the house, we would climb a short hand-built wooden ladder into the hay loft above the cow's stall. That was where Grandpa kept three fifty-gallon oak barrels of red wine that he tapped off three larger barrels down below between the manger and the hen house. Grandpa would take a tin cup off a little shelf above the wine barrels, thrust the cup under the spigot of one of the barrels, open the spigot and fill the cup with wine.

"Gotta test it for flavor occasionally," he would say, winking at me conspiratorially.

I always thought if I forgot everything else about grandma and grandpa's, it would be okay as long as I didn't forget the delicious smell of hay and cow and chickens and red wine all mixed up together.

That was a fragrance more precious than perfume, even Candace's perfume. If I concentrated hard enough and inhaled deeply enough, I could recall that smell almost anytime, as if I were sitting right there in that hay loft at that very moment.

I visited grandpa's barn in my memory whenever I needed a respite from the mayhem around me. That barn was my private inner sanctum; a center of gentle calm in a world of raucous noise and chaos.

Grandpa didn't talk much while testing his cup of wine. He would lift the cup to his nose, sniff its wonderful redolent bouquet, sip, swish the tannic brew around in his mouth, and swallow and groan with great satisfaction. He savored his liquid red refreshment as if he were recalling the whole process of picking the grapes, mashing them and fermenting the juice or as if he were recalling his early days in Italy.

I was content to sit silently and watch him, glad to share his private joy and to ruminate on a few thoughts and memories of my own. At times like that I felt sorry for kids who didn't have grandpas who owned barns.

Having drunk his wine, my grandpa would stand up and we would climb back down the ladder, gather up the milk pail and head into the house. Once in the house, grandpa would reach out to an electric switch just inside the back door and turn on the electric fence so the cow wouldn't stray out of the pasture.

"Watch out for that fence," grandpa often warned me. "It'll zap you if you aren't paying attention."

I knew too, from personal experience that my grandpa wasn't kidding. I remembered the time Web had forgotten the fence was turned on and had decided to grab hold of it to climb over it rather than unlock the gate. I had laughed so hard at Web dancing around grabbing at himself; I thought I was going to throw up.

I noticed there was smoke coming from the chimney of the house. My grandparents were up. Of course they were almost always up early in the morning, even in retirement.

"Everybody grab something and carry it into the house," mom said.

I helped Grace straggle out of the car, then went around to the back of the station wagon and extricated Genie and a suitcase, and started up the path to the house, following my mom and Loretta, with the other little kids hard on my heels.

Web was still at the car unloading Christmas presents. I would have to go back and help him, I knew, but first, I wanted to see grandpa and grandma.

Loretta banged on the front door. Seconds later, there was grandpa and grandma saying, "Come in, come in." and giving us all hugs and kisses.

As soon as I received my full quota of hugs and kisses, I retreated back to the car to help Web. Us two men then finished unloading the station wagon and deposited the unloaded items where they were supposed to go.

When you walked in the front door of grandma and grandpa's house, you were immediately confronted by wide wooden stairs that climbed up to aunt Gizzy's and aunt Jeannie's bedrooms. To the right was another door that opened into the main living room. A big brick fireplace dominated the living room. Beyond the living room, at the west end of the house you would find the parlor.

Grandpa and grandma's bedroom was tucked next to the parlor and living room, on the south side of the house. The indoor bathroom contained a sink and a tub. The toilet was in a room of its own, inconveniently located out on the back porch. One unfortunate feature of grandpa and grandma's house was that it could be a long cold trip to the toilet room in the middle of the night.

I almost always had to use the toilet in the middle of the night. To get to it I had to traipse down the stairs through the living room, along the short hallway to the family room and out the back door. The toilet room was heated by a portable plug-in heater in the winter, but it wasn't much help. It barely managed to keep the water in the toilet bowl from freezing. It did not keep my backside from freezing to the toilet lid.

The east end of the house contained the family room, dining area and kitchen, and the pantry where grandma kept jars and jars and jars of cherries, peaches, pears, corn, green beans, red beans, meat and whatever else she managed to can during the previous summer.Web and my mom's suitcase and things were dropped off in the parlor where they would be sleeping, Loretta and the girl's things were stowed in Aunt Gizzy's room upstairs. My stuff and the little boys' stuff were thrown in a heap in Aunt Jeannie's room. Aunt Jeannie would sleep with the other girls in Aunt Gizzy's room. Our Christmas presents were piled up in the living room near where the Christmas tree would soon be erected. It was a tradition in grandpa and grandma's house that the Christmas tree wasn't put up until the day before Christmas Eve.

When suitcases and packages and paraphernalia were deposited where they needed to go, it was time to join grandpa and grandma in the family room around the big wood heating stove. This was the usual gathering area for the family. The living room was saved for more formal occasions and the parlor was primarily used for watching television or working on jigsaw puzzles and sewing.

The smell of coffee permeated the air. Grandpa sat down at the south end of a big walnut dining table. Grandma took a seat in a corner at the other end of the table and next to a built-in china hutch. She started making toast in a toaster, which sat on a rolling cart that also included the electric coffee pot and various condiments. Mom pulled up a chair at the end of the table near grandma. Web parked himself next to the wood stove.

Aunt Jeannie and us kids scattered on miscellaneous chairs or on the floor around the wood stove. Aunt Gizzy, a teacher at a high school in Portland, was engaged to be married and grandma said she was going to stay in Portland and spend Christmas with her fiancés family.

A happy hubbub of conversation soon burbled merrily, like thick soup in a stew pot, everybody trying to talk at once, and everybody trying to talk louder than the next person. The first item of conversation, of course, was the weather and the flooding rivers.

"I'm afraid we're in for some flooding right here in Cedar Grove if the MacKenzie keeps rising," grandma said.

"At least we're high and dry here on this hill," grandpa said.

"Yes," grandma agreed, "but the homes and farms along the river probably are going to have to be evacuated. I just hope there's no loss of life."

Web related how we'd almost driven off into the Umpqua River then, but I noticed that my mom did not say anything about the near fatal accident with the truck, and nobody else said anything about it either. The conversation eventually turned to grandpa and grandma marveling about the growth of their grandchildren.

"My Francis, how you've grown since we saw you last," grandma said.

"I'm five-ten now," I said. "I think I'm going to be at least six feet tall."

"You in high school yet?" grandpa asked, slurping coffee from his cup while he looked me over.

"I hope to start in January." I said, casting an eye toward my mom to see if this fit in with her plans.

"Gonna play football?" grandpa asked.

"It's too late this year, but I hope to be able to play next year," I said.

"Football's a pretty tough game," grandpa said. "Think you're tough enough?"

"I'm pretty tough," I said.

"I just bet you are," grandpa said, winking at me.

"I've been working out a lot on the weights you gave me," I said.

"We'll have to see how Francis' health is before we can consider letting him play sports dad," my mom said.

I knew she would say that! Anger and bitterness boiled up in me, but I managed to dismiss them quickly because I was in a happy place and I didn't want bad thoughts to disrupt my good mood.

"I could probably play baseball this year," I said, looking at my mom defiantly. "I'd really like to do that."

"We'll talk about it when the time comes," mom said.

"Can you hit the ball pretty good?" grandpa asked me.

"I hit home runs all the time in eighth grade, before I got sick," I said.

By the time the conversation turned to gossip about relatives living in the area, my stomach was talking to me. I had also smelled fried eggs and bacon, grandpa's usual breakfast, when we walked into the house, and the smell had stuck with me and now I was ravenous. My hunger must have shown, because just about then my grandpa said, "We better get these young ones some food."

The younger kids were satisfied with cold cereal. I, however, asked for and received permission to fix myself some bacon and eggs.

"You cook pretty good?" grandpa inquired.

"Francis is a very good cook," my mom said.

I fried myself some bacon, then cracked two fresh brown eggs into the hot bacon grease and spooned the grease over the eggs until the yolks turned cloudy on top. Grandma had made a pile of toast and set that and some homemade strawberry jelly on the dining table. I dug into my breakfast, relishing every last morsel. When I finished my bacon and eggs, it was time for some of grandma's canned cherries.

"You know where they are," grandma said. "Help yourself."

I retrieved two quart jars of canned cherries from the pantry, as the other kids had decided they wanted cherries too. The pantry was a small room at the north end of the kitchen. It shared a kind of closed-in back porch with the wood bin. Rain coats and boots were kept here, along with grandma's brooms and other household paraphernalia.

The pantry was about six feet wide and eight feet deep and lined all around with twelve-inch wide pine board shelves. Each shelf was heavily burdened with quart jars, either Mason or Ball. Grandma didn't play favorites. She just bought whatever jars were on sale when she needed them. The jars were either clear or tinted green. They contained cherries, peaches, pears, corn, peas, string beans, mincemeat, salami, beans – anything grandma could can, she did. I always wished I had the talent to draw a picture of grandma's pantry, because I liked color and it was so colorful with its reds and greens and yellows and oranges.

Sometimes, when I entered the pantry, I just stood there for a few minutes marveling at the bounty of preserved food spread before me. I ate two huge helpings of red Bing Cherries before I quit. Once everybody had eaten breakfast, it was time to plan out the rest of the day.

"I have to go downtown sometime today and do a little more shopping." grandma said.

"I'd like to lie down and go to sleep for a little while," mom said.

Web agreed that he could use a little "shut eye" too. I was afraid my parents would insist that me and the other kids lay down and sleep awhile too. No way did I want to miss any part of what might happen that day. I was tired, but I could sleep later.

Aunt Jeannie said she would like to go visit some of other her friends who were home from college like she was. I kind of wished I could go with Jeannie, except that would mean I would have to sit around and listen to a lot of girl talk. I liked it when Gizzy and Jeannie's girlfriends flirted with me, but I usually got pretty bored when there was nothing but girl talk to listen to.

Fortunately, grandma asked if she could take me and Loretta to town with her. "Maybe you can get the little ones to lie down for awhile," she said to mom.

Grandpa and I went out to the barn and retrieved some eggs and performed a few other chores before we left for town. Grandpa chopped kindling and I helped carry it into the house and placed it in the wood bin in the pantry. Grandma and Loretta were just finishing up the dishes.

Once the chores were finished, Loretta and I trundled into grandpa and grandma's old '49 Ford with them. As soon as we were all seated in the car grandma began telling grandpa how to drive. Grandma had never held a driver's license herself, but it obviously was her opinion that grandpa was not a good enough driver without a little direction from her.

They sat in the front seat, grandpa wearing his battered old grey fedora hat and a jacket, and grandma wearing her black box hat with fishnet, and a long winter coat. Grandma's long gray/black hair was tied back in a severe bun. She was so tall and thin I wondered how my mom and my aunts ended up being so chubby.

"Be careful backing out of here Alphonse," grandma warned. "Web and Mary Catherine's car's back there you know."

"I know it's back there," grandpa said good-naturedly. "You just watch the scenery and I'll watch the road."

He never seemed to let grandma's telling him how to drive ruffle his feathers; most of the time he just ignored her.

Still, there was some justification for grandma's telling grandpa how to drive. He was infamous in Cedar Grove for his lack of attention behind the wheel. He often ran stop signs, followed other cars too closely and seldom, if ever, signaled lane changes or turns. By some miracle he had never been involved in a traffic accident and even more miraculous, he'd never been nailed with a traffic ticket. Grandpa led a charmed life, like Mister Magoo, or Froggy in *Wind in the Willows*, which exasperated grandma to no end.

If her husband had received even one teensy little traffic ticket, I think her belief that he was a bad risk driver would have been justified and she could have nagged him without remorse.

"But no," she always said, "God watches out for little children and old fools."

On this particular trip downtown, grandpa didn't seem to notice the train moving south to north on the railroad tracks at the intersection of Cedar Grove Avenue and Main Street. The train wasn't moving very fast, in fact, it was inching its way along in a switching maneuver. There were no crossing arms with flashing lights in Cedar Grove. Automobile drivers were just supposed to watch for trains and be careful.

Grandpa drove across the tracks barely even giving the moving train as much as a sidelong glance. I usually was not bothered by grandpa's driving, but when I saw the cow-catcher on the front of the train in ever-sharpening detail as it crept closer and closer to the side of the vehicle I was sitting in, I became a little nervous. Loretta even squeaked out a little warning cry of, "grandpa!" but grandpa hardly seemed to notice anything unusual.

"Alphonse, you almost killed us," grandma scolded, whacking grandpa on the arm with her purse as we rattled over the railroad tracks and onto the safety of the other side of the street.

"Whadya' talkin' about?" grandpa said. "I had plenty of time."

Grandma shrugged her shoulders in defeat. We were safe for now anyway.

"The first place I want to go is Staley's Department Store," she said.

Grandpa maneuvered the '49 Ford along Main Street until we arrived at Staley's. The curb in front was lined with vehicles.

"Go around back to the parking lot," grandma directed. Grandpa did as he was told.

When he had parked in back of Staley's grandma said, "You kids come with me, grandpa can stay here and smoke his pipe if he wants to."

Grandpa seemed to approve of that plan and he reached into his upper coat pocket for his pipe. Loretta and I followed grandma into Staley's.

"Whatcha' gonna' get here grandma?" Loretta inquired.

"Well," grandma said, surprising us, "I thought I would buy my two grandchildren their Christmas presents.

"Right now, grandma?" I asked.

"Why not? We're here," grandma said. "Less you got some objection."

Loretta and I agreed that we had no objections. We were just amazed that our grandma was doing this. It was almost totally uncharacteristic of her. Even when we were very small and living with her and grandpa while our mom went through a nasty divorce with our real father, grandma had never shown this kind of spontaneity.

"What would you like for Christmas?" grandma asked, looking at each of us inquiringly. "I haven't had time to get you anything yet and I don't want to forget."

I thought about what I wanted most – something baseball oriented of course. But grandma had brought us to a department store where the featured item was clothing. I remembered my dream about finding Jesus in the forest and how his cape had turned into a red jacket when he put it on me. I suddenly knew what to ask for. "I could use a new jacket," I said.

In fact, I really would like a new jacket, I decided. I still was wearing the one I'd worn in eighth grade and it just didn't strike me as the kind of jacket a cool high school guy wore. It was a little tattered looking too. My parents hadn't had a lot of money to buy me new clothes since my bout with rheumatic fever.

Like I said, I would have preferred a Mickey Mantle autographed centerfielder's glove, but that surely was out of the question. Grandma probably would have thought that wasn't practical enough. She guided us to the clothing section of Staley's.

"Can I help you Mrs. Granatelli?" a friendly female clerk asked.

"We're looking for a jacket for this young man," grandma said, indicating me with a caressing hand on my shoulder. "This is my grandson Francis," she announced proudly.

I was amazed again. I'd never heard my grandma speak so proudly of me to another person. I loved my grandma and she had just made me feel like I was the most special person in the whole world.

"What size do you wear?" the clerk asked me.

"Large," I told her.

"Large," she repeated, sizing me up. She apparently agreed that I knew my own size and pulled a couple of jackets from a rack and held them out to grandma and me for inspection.

One was an olive green corduroy coat and the other was a red nylon ski jacket. Of course, I felt instantly drawn toward the red jacket. Red was my favorite color. Besides, I remembered that Jesus had told me in my dream that whenever I wore his red cape that he would be with me and protect me and give me courage. Surely a red jacket was the next best thing.

I tried to act nonchalant when trying the jacket on, but it fit just right and I knew in my heart it was destined to be mine. It was going to be my lucky jacket. I hoped it didn't cost too much. I admired my sporty image in a full length mirror on the wall as long as I could without seeming too vain. Truth is, I thought that jacket perfectly complemented my blue jeans, tennis shoes and checkered flannel shirt.

It made my waist look thinner, my shoulders broader, my eyes bluer, my dark, wavy hair wavier. It was warm too. It made me feel very special. I thought to myself, "Eat your heart out James Dean."

"You like that jacket?" grandma asked.

"I like it," I croaked in appreciation.

"Turn around and cross your arms over your chest," the clerk directed me. I did as I was told.

"Seems to be plenty roomy," the clerk reported to grandma. "Red's the color of courage, you know."

"How are the sleeves," grandma asked. "Are they long enough, too long?"

"Just right," I announced happily.

"You want this jacket then?" grandma asked. "You don't want to try any others on?"

"This is the one for me," I said happily.

I couldn't believe grandma was going to buy that jacket for me, but then she said those three magic words, "We'll take it."

I was in a dazed fog after that and couldn't for the life of me pay much attention to whatever Loretta was picking out for her gift. When our purchases were paid for, grandma led us back out to the car where grandpa was puffing happily on his pipe and wishing everyone who came within a hundred yards of his car a Merry Christmas. When he saw my new jacket he said, "Well look at that now. I never seen anything so red in my entire life. That's a smart looking jacket. Maybe I'll just trade you this ol' denim thing I'm wearing."

"Doesn't he look handsome in it," grandma cooed.

"Handsome!" Grandma had never said anything like that about me that I could remember.

"I think he's just about the best looking grandkid in this here town," grandpa said. "I think we're gonna' have to look out for the girls though. Soon as they see Francis in this getup they're gonna' be swarmin' all over the place."

The rest of the morning was more of the same. Everywhere we stopped, grandpa and grandma bragged about me. They probably bragged about Loretta too, but I didn't hear that. When we stopped at the feed store to buy a salt lick for Bess and some feed for the chickens, grandpa showed me and my new red jacket off to the people who worked at the feed store.

When I accompanied grandma into the Safeway store, she introduced me with obvious pride to the butcher and the cashier and any other acquaintances she saw. I wasn't sure which was most red as we started to drive home, me or my red jacket. But I sure liked all the attention.

More than once that morning I wondered if my new red jacket might be a symbol of something larger.

I could not shake the thought that it might be more than mere coincidence that my favorite color was red, that Cardinal's vestments were red, and that Staley's just happened to stock a red jacket that fit me like this one did. Back at grandpa and grandma's house mom, Web, Aunt Jeannie and my other sisters and brothers all admired my new jacket.

"Did you remember to thank your grandmother properly?" mom asked?

"I sure did," I said.

"If you take good care of this jacket it should last you a couple of years," mom said.

That was my mom's goal for all of my wearing apparel. Everything should last long enough to spread the cost out over at least two years. That must take away the sting of the purchase price, I reasoned. I didn't know how much the jacket had cost grandma, but I guessed it was in the area of forty dollars. Even I knew that was a princely sum for someone living on Social Security.

"I'll take real good care of my jacket," I promised. "I'll guard it with my life." I meant what I said too. I just didn't know it would be so hard to keep my promise and that my life might be saved by the courage that jacket gave me.

CHAPTER VIII

I t was lunchtime. Grandma and mom made sandwiches and set them out on the dining table. Jars of canned fruit were opened and set out. Homemade marshmallow fudge that grandma had cooked was set out. Cookies that mom had baked joined the feast. A box of chocolate covered cherries, sugar and frosting-coated walnuts and several other kinds of nuts, shelled and unshelled, were added for good measure. Everybody ate heartily, devouring the sandwiches and the canned fruit then digging into the sweets. Grandma brewed a fresh pot of coffee. Grandpa dug into the storage closet underneath the stairs and brought out a gallon jug of his homemade wine. As he was pouring himself and Web a glass of wine, mom looked on apprehensively. She did not want Web to get drunk.

The irony of grandpa accidentally serving his guests too much wine was not lost on me. Because Grandpa had grown up drinking wine he thought nothing of imbibing several glasses a day. But he never got drunk and never was unpleasant to be around. If anything, the more wine he drank, the more fun grandpa was. His tales about Italy and his early days in Oregon grew taller and funnier in direct proportion to the amount of wine he drank.

He knew instinctively, and from early childhood training, how to sip a glass of wine and nurse it along and how to thoroughly enjoy it. The problem was, he was so proud to serve his friends and visitors as much wine as they could drink, they sometimes couldn't handle it. Grandpa's hospitality knew no bounds, but he hated it when people got drunk on his wine, and occasionally they did.

Grandma had told grandpa that other people weren't always able to hold their liquor like he was, but it didn't seem to register with him. I loved grandpa so much whatever he did was okay with me. But I also shared mom's anxiety about Web drinking. More than once since Web and my mom had been married I'd had to intervene in their spats to keep Web from hurting her. Web was a totally different person when he'd had too much to drink.

The last time Web had drunk too much and turned mean had been during a summer camping trip a couple of years earlier.

A beautiful weekend of camping by the pristine Truckee River in the Sierra Nevada foothills of California had been ruined when Web and mom began arguing. The fight escalated to the point I had to insert myself between them to protect my mom and I threw a large rock at Web to stop his menacing advance toward her. I could remember how scared I'd been when the rock hit Web in the chest and Web roared, "I'm going to beat the crap out of you kid."

"Better me than my mom," I had retorted.

But I had not relished the idea of being beat up. Then my mom grabbed Web's shotgun out of the car and pointed it at him. I don't know if I've ever been as scared as I was during that tense moment. The loud snap of the trigger hammer clicking into firing position echoed through the woods like the sound of sudden death. It stilled even the chatter of the squirrels.

Fortunately, Web decided to sulk off with another beer. He fell asleep under a fir tree as he sipped his beer and when he woke up he was apologetic, promising he would never let himself get that out of control again.

I didn't know if I believed him. I know my mother didn't believe him.

The potential for trouble always lurked just beneath the surface of our family's apparent tranquility. Grandpa had no idea that he might be fueling another fire. The rest of the morning was uneventful, however. Web did get a little tipsy, but the cordial atmosphere of grandpa and grandma's home seemed to work enough magic on him that he didn't sink into one of his alcoholic funks. In fact, after a couple glasses of wine, he moseyed off to the parlor to lay down for a nap, and soon, the whole family could hear deep snoring coming from that direction. Grandpa shuffled off to take a nap shortly after Web did and pretty soon the two of them were snoring in virtual concert, "rumbling the rafters," as grandma put it.

About that time Jeannie came home from visiting her friends and announced that it was time to go to Blessed Redeemer Church and decorate for midnight mass. Loretta and I got to tag along.

We actually decorated the church's school auditorium. The church had built a new elementary school, kindergarten through sixth grade, across the parking lot from the sanctuary and the school had just been operating a few months. Grandma told us that Father Shanahan, the parish priest, wanted to hold midnight mass in the school auditorium to give parishioners a look at the new facility.

Three nuns already were working in the auditorium when we arrived. They introduced themselves to Loretta and I as Sister Grace, Sister Will and Sister Rowena. All three were wearing their black habits so it was hard at first to distinguish one from the other.

I did notice that Sister Grace was short and had a chubby face, pink cheeks, a red nose and tiny, darting blue eyes. Sister Will was taller than Sister Grace and had a thin face with bifocal glasses perched halfway down her aquiline nose. I noticed that she tended to peer at people over the top of her glasses, giving her a rather intimidating owlish look. Sister Will appeared to be the oldest of the trio. Her hands were very wrinkled and she moved slowly and seemed to tire easily. Sister Rowena was young, of medium height, and had a pretty face with smooth soft skin and big brown eyes. I noticed that the fingers of her hands were long and pretty and I wondered if she played the piano. All three of the sisters were teachers at the school.

One thing I hadn't realized about nuns before that meeting was that they were real people. The only time I'd ever been around nuns was when I attended a Catholic Church service and during those times I had never gotten close enough to actually talk to them.

These three nuns chatted and giggled and bickered as they worked, just like my mom and grandma and aunts and sisters. Sister Rowena engaged me in conversation as I helped her string crepe paper ribbons across the auditorium. I told her I hoped to become a baseball player someday and she asked me what team I liked best.

"The Yankees," I told her.

"Ah. The Yankees," she said, nodding as if she understood. "They know how to win don't they?"

"Yeah," I said, "Except in the World Series."

"They lost the World Series again this year?" Sister Rowena asked sympathetically. "Who'd they play?"

"The St. Louis Cardinals," I said. "But at least they only lost to the Cardinals by one game. Last year they were swept four straight by the Los Angeles Dodgers."

"I remember," Sister Rowena said. "Sandy Koufax was pretty tough on them wasn't he?"

"He set a league record for strikeouts," I reminded her. "He won game four too."

"Dandy Don was pretty hard on the Yanks too, wasn't he?" Sister Rosena said.

"Who?"

"The Big D. Don Drysdale."

"Yeah, he was." I said. "He won game three. The M and M Boys couldn't do much against Koufax and Drysdale."

"The M and M Boys." Sister Rowena said. "You mean Mickey Mantle and Roger Maris? I think they were too worn out after the '61 season when they were chasing Babe Ruth's homerun record," Sister Rowena said.

"Musta' been something like that," I agreed.

"Mantle's one of the best homerun hitters ever and Maris eventually did break Ruth's homerun record."

"I like Willie Mays," Sister Grace said from the top of a stepladder. "Say hey!"

She said "Say hey" with such force she almost fell off the ladder. That set her to laughing.

"Oh, I almost made an error," she giggled.

The other nuns laughed at that.

"You know a lot about baseball," I said to Sister Rowena.

"I have three brothers," she said. "They all played at school. It was pretty hard to grow up in my house and not know something about baseball."

"Do the Giants still play in Brooklyn?" Sister Will asked, attempting to join in the conversation.

"The Giants play in San Francisco," Sister Grace laughed. "They left New York in the fifties. Besides, it was the Dodgers who played in Brooklyn."

"Are the Dodgers still in Brooklyn?" Sister Will asked.

"The Dodgers moved to Los Angeles about the same time the Giants moved to San Francisco," Sister Rowena said gently.

"You know that Laurel and Hardy skit about who's on first?" Sister Grace asked me.

"I've seen the movie," I said. "It's pretty funny."

"It's hilarious," Sister Grace said.

"Wasn't it Abbott and Costello who did who's on first?" Sister Rowena pointed out.

"Oh yeah," I said. "That's who I saw do it in the movie."

"You ever heard that joke about the baseball player who prayed for a grand salami?" Sister Grace asked me.

"I don't think so," I said.

"Well," Sister Grace said, "this batter had gone hitless for several weeks. He was in a terrible slump."

"He came up to bat in the bottom of the ninth with the score tied, two outs, and the bases loaded in a big playoff game that would determine if his team went to the World Series."

"Before he steps up to the plate he prays to God to send him a grand salami. God says, 'Okay, no problem.'"

"The batter is facing a full count, three and two, and he's getting pretty nervous, but then he thinks to himself, God said everything would be okay, just swing hard at the next pitch and the ball will fly."

"The batter swings as hard as he can at the next pitch. Sure enough, the ball flies toward the outfield fence. It looks like a grand slam home run alright. But all of a sudden, the opposing team's centerfielder leaps high in the air, extends his glove over the fence, and catches the ball for an out to send the game into extra innings."

"The batter comes back to his team's dugout really angry. 'Why did you promise me a grand salami, then let the ball get caught?' he asks God.

"The salami's hanging in your locker," God says. "And if I may say so it certainly is a grand one. How about that centerfielder though? Did he make a great catch or what?"

Sister Grace doubled over with laughter when she delivered the punch line. She infected Sister Will and Sister Rowena and they infected Jeannie and the rest of us. We were laughing so hard, when Father Shanahan walked in he started laughing too and he didn't even know why.

Things finally turned more sober and we worked diligently at stringing garland and hanging red paper bells around the room. Then I assisted Father Shanahan and the janitor, a Mr. Chavez, in setting metal folding chairs out in long rows before a makeshift stage that had been placed at the front of the auditorium. A wooden altar would be brought over from the church in time for Midnight Mass, I learned.

Father Shanahan was a physically imposing man, even in his black priest suit. He stood at least six feet tall and weighed at least two hundred pounds. His hair was wavy and reddish-orange and his skin was white and freckled. Not only was he impressive physically, he spoke Spanish to Mr. Chavez from time to time, to help Mr. Chavez understand how things needed to be laid out, and I thought that was pretty cool.

While we worked, Father Shanahan revealed that he had grown up in Boston and that he was a Boston Red Sox fan.

"Too bad they lost the Babe," he said.

"You mean Babe Ruth?" I asked.

"The one and only," Father Shanahan said.

"I didn't know Babe Ruth played for Boston," I said.

"Oh yes," Father Shanahan said. "When the Sox lost him their fortunes turned sour and they haven't been the same since."

"Wow," I said. "Babe Ruth."

Father Shanahan later told me he started seminary when he was eighteen and had been a priest for thirty years.

"What made you decide to become a priest?" I asked.

"God called me to become one," he said.

"How did you know God was calling you?" I asked.

"I didn't at first," Father Shanahan said. "I was a lot like you when I was growing up. My family was catholic. My grandmother wanted me to become a priest. But I had mixed feelings about it."

"What made you decide?"

"I attended seminary and found out. I visited Saint Martin's College Seminary in Cleveland and decided to go there after graduation from high school."

"What is seminary exactly?" I asked. "I've heard about it, but don't really know anything about it."

"Seminary is like college," Father Shanahan explained, "though not quite like a regular college."

"At seminary, under the direction of the Rector and Spiritual Director, you pray and meditate a lot. You take religious studies and philosophy classes, study the Bible and learn Latin and Greek."

"What if you don't think you're cut out to be a priest?" I asked, suddenly conjuring up a vision of Candy Reulmann.

"That's why you go to seminary. At seminary, you learn if you are suited to modeling your life after Jesus, who was both servant and leader."

"You do a lot of volunteer work with community agencies, visiting people in the hospital and in nursing homes, working in soup kitchens, working with minority groups, young people and so on. That way, you learn what gifts God has given you and how to use them."

"But what if a person goes to seminary and still decides he doesn't want to become a priest? Is it too late to change your mind?"

"Of course not."

"I don't think I could be a priest," I said.

"It can be a tough job," Father Shanahan admitted. "But the rewards far outweigh the drawbacks."

"But why don't you think you could be a priest?" he asked.

"I don't know," I said. "I just don't think I'm . . ."

"Good enough?"

"Exactly," I said. "Plus I don't know if I have enough faith."

I felt totally guilty about my thoughts of Candy right then.

"Who *is* good enough or faithful enough to serve God?" Father Shanahan asked. He searched my eyes with a piercing look similar to the one Jesus had given me. I wished people wouldn't do that.

"You know," Father Shanahan continued, "if God only looked for perfect people to become priests there probably wouldn't be any priests. The real glory of God is more often displayed in less than perfect people who simply believe in him and follow his holy bidding in spite of their many flaws."

"I suppose," I said.

"Don't worry," Father Shanahan said. "God won't make you do something you really don't want to do."

"What about Jonah?" I asked. "He didn't want to preach in Nineveh, but God made him."

"I suspect Jonah secretly wanted to do that," Father Shanahan insisted. We all want to be heroes deep down in our hearts, but most of us think we don't possess the necessary qualities."

"God's most reluctant servants often turn out to be our greatest heroes because once God's Holy Spirit enters into our hearts, we start wanting to be good and to do good and believing – with his help – that we can."

"Maybe," I said tentatively.

"Take Moses," Father Shanahan said. "He was a murderer, yet God chose him to lead the Jews out of Egypt. He tried to talk God out of using him, but God's Holy Spirit entered his heart and he became a hero and did much good in spite of his initial reluctance."

"Take David," Father Shanahan continued. "He was afraid to fight Goliath, but God gave him courage and later gave him King Saul's throne. God loved David so much he even forgave him when he committed the sin of adultery with Bathsheba."

"Take Saint Matthew. He was a despised tax collector before Jesus called him to be one of his disciples."

"And then there was Paul, who used to kill Jews, and God struck him blind on the road to Damascus. Paul became one of the greatest disciples of all time."

"Okay, I give up," I said laughing. Father Shanahan was so – adamant.

"But I still don't think I'm cut out to be a priest," I insisted. I could be adamant too.

"Maybe, maybe not," Father Shanahan said. "Only time will tell. You are a first-born son, however, and first-born sons are very special to our Holy Father. Then there's that whole business of you being saved from death. God saved you for some reason you know?"

I frantically waved my red jacket out the window. But it was still too dark and the helicopter pilot didn't appear to see us. Either he was concentrating too hard looking for survivors in the river or he couldn't see us inside the house. The helicopter roared over the house and up the river.

"What are we going to do?" Ronnie asked desperately. "What if it doesn't come back?"

"It has to come back," I said just as desperately.

I wasn't sure I really believed what I was saying, but I was trying hard to be positive.

"They have to have been notified by now that we're missing," Ronnie reasoned.

"I wish I knew what to do," I said. "If we stay in this house the helicopter pilot might never see us. If we take our chances on jumping into the river we might be swept away and killed."

"We have to do something," Ronnie agreed. "But Francis, I'm scared."

"I'm scared too Ronnie," I admitted. "But I believe Jesus is with us. We have to be brave."

Finally, we made a decision.

We agreed to try pushing the dresser out the window. We thought it would float okay with the drawers out of it – at least for a few minutes – and the drawer wells would give us handholds. Once we were in the water, we'd hang on to the dresser and kick and paddle our way over to the bank. It sounded pretty crazy, but we didn't know what else to do and it might just be insane enough to work. Still, we tried to talk ourselves out of swimming for it.

"I agree with you that I don't think we could just stay here in the house until the river recedes," Ronnie said. "If the rain would stop it might not take more than a couple of days for the river to recede enough the house would stop traveling, but who knows if that will happen."

"Maybe we could stay here," I said. "I don't have any experience with floods. But we don't know when the rain might stop and by then it might be too late for us to be rescued."

"You're right," Ronnie said.

"I don't know if I am or not," I admitted. "I just feel like we ought to try to save ourselves."

"Let's see if we can push the dresser out the window," Ronnie said summoning up her courage. "We better hurry because the helicopter could come back any minute."

"But how are we going to keep the dresser from floating away until we jump in the water?" she asked.

"Shoot," I said. "I never thought of that."

"What if we hooked some of dad's belts together and tied them to the dresser?" Ronnie asked.

"Does he have enough belts?"

"About half a dozen I bet," Ronnie said

"I don't know if that will be enough," I said, looking at the dresser and mentally calculating how far below the bedroom window the river flowed.

"Does your dad have very many neckties?" I asked.

"He has lots of neckties!" Ronnie said excitedly.

"Quick," I said. "Let's knot them together with the belts. I hear the helicopter coming back again."

We frantically knotted about twenty of Ronnie's father's ties and his half dozen belts together. Lucky for us Doctor Mailer wore ties almost everyday and owned so many. We tied our daisy chain to the dresser.

"We better tie the other end of this rope we've made to the bed post," I said. "I'm not sure we can hold onto the dresser once we push it out the window."

"Good idea," Ronnie said. "Do you think we have enough length?"

"I figure we've got about twenty feet," I said. "I figure it's about five feet to the water and maybe three feet to the bed. That gives us maybe 12 feet to spare. I don't want the dresser to drift too far from the house."

I looked out the window at the river. "Only one way to find out," I said looking into Ronnie's eyes.

I saw nothing but resolution and bravery in Ronnie's eyes. My heart swelled with love. The whup, whup, whup was right above us again, then it moved on up the river. I hoped the helicopter pilot would make a few more passes over the house so we would have time to put out plan into action I asked Ronnie is she was ready to go.

"I guess so," she said.

She looked into my eyes and took my hand then said, "Francis, I just want to tell you how much I like you and admire you and I hope you feel the same way about me."

"I do Ronnie," I said. "I do."

"I've been praying to God and to Saint Christopher to watch over us," Ronnie said.

"I believe in the power of prayer," I said.

I wanted to give Ronnie hope, and I did believe. We held each other a minute and I bent down and kissed her forehead. Then it was time. I lifted the front end of the dresser up to the window sill, then went around to the other end and helped Ronnie push it out the window. The dresser hurtled downward and splashed into the water below. The line we'd fashioned out of old ties and belts played out quickly and I feared it wouldn't be long enough after all, or wouldn't hold. To my surprise, it was long enough and it did hold.

"Boy, getting rescued sure is hard work," I said. "It never looks this tough in the movies."

Ronnie laughed. Then she exclaimed, "Francis! You're arm is bleeding again."

"No time to worry about it now," I said. "We've got to go."

At that point the sobering realization that we both could die in the next few minutes struck us full force. Once we jumped into the river we might not ever see each other again.

"I guess this is it," Ronnie said.

"I guess."

"Francis?"

"Be careful when you jump out the window that you don't hit the dresser or those jagged brackets sticking up," I said with a huge lump in my throat. "It's still pretty dark out there and you might get hurt."

"I'm afraid," Ronnie said, her voice quavering.

"Me too," I said, "But we've got to do this."

"I can hear the helicopter coming back and who knows how many more passes the pilot will make?"

"I know," Ronnie said. "Look, would you go first so you can grab me when I hit the water?"

"Sure," I said. "You promise you'll come? You can't stay here."

"I'll come," Ronnie promised.

I pulled my red jacket on even though it was still somewhat soggy and climbed into the window.

"Jesus," I prayed out loud, looking at Ronnie. "We sure could use your help right now. The Bible says faith is the assurance of things hoped for and the conviction of things not seen. You said in my dream that I would be protected whenever I wore my red jacket. I'm thanking you now for saving us. Amen."

"Francis!" Ronnie cried anxiously.

"Bye Ronnie," I said. "I love you."

I looked at her, trying to drink her face in so I would remember it for the rest of my life – however short that might be.

CHAPTER XIV

I pushed off and jumped into the boiling brown water below, praying I wouldn't hit the dresser or some other floating object and knock myself out or land so far away I wouldn't be able to grab hold of the dresser. Miraculously, I landed right next to the dresser and managed to grab hold of it as soon as I broke through the surface of the water. The river was icy cold and a total shock to my system.

"Come on!" I yelled up at Ronnie. "I'll catch hold of you."

She jumped without hesitation and I was struck again by how brave she was. She possessed an inner strength that I hadn't seen in many girls my age and I knew she would be alright if she just survived this day. Ronnie splashed down right next to me and I grabbed her shirt as she went under the water. She came up sputtering.

"Oh, my gosh it's cold!"

I couldn't help laughing. She looked like a kitten that had fallen into a bathtub.

"You're laughing," she said, punching me in the arm.

"Sorry," I said. "I can't help it. You just look so darn cute all wet like that."

But there wasn't much time for joking around. I could hear the helicopter coming again and I was determined this time that the pilot should see us.

"Quick!" I told Ronnie. "Help me untie the rope so we can float out into the river. We'll have a better chance of being seen."

But it wasn't as easy to untie the rope as I had figured. The knots had snugged up really tight when the dresser fell, and our hands were wet and cold. Fortunately, I still had what was left of my pocket knife in my jeans. I pulled the knife out and sawed at the rope as fast as I could with the leftover stub of the blade. It seemed to take way longer than it should have to cut through one of Doctor Mailer's silk ties, but I finally succeeded.

"Oh!" Ronnie exclaimed. "We're floating away."

"It's okay," I said, trying to reassure both of us. "Let's kick our feet and try to steer ourselves toward the shore."

I looked up and saw the helicopter coming. Ronnie helped me struggle out of my jacket and I waved it with one hand the best I could. I did not want to totally let go of the dresser.

"I think he's seen us!" Ronnie said excitedly.

Sure enough, the helicopter pilot shined his searchlight directly upon us. Then we could see him waving. After a minute, he flew off up the river."

"Why's he leaving?" Ronnie asked.

"I think maybe he's going to tell someone on the ground that he found us," I said. "They'll probably send a boat out and he'll guide them to us."

"At least that's what I'm hoping," I added.

"Oh, Francis? Are we saved? Are we truly saved?" Ronnie asked.

"I hope so," I said. "We should know in a few minutes."

Just then Ronnie spotted two little kids, a boy and a girl, clinging to the roof of a dog house, maybe fifty yards downstream.

They were screaming for help and looked like they didn't have the will to hang on much longer. When they saw Ronnie and me, however, they seemed to perk up and directed their screaming at us.

"Help us! Please help!" they pleaded.

"Oh Francis, we've got to help them," Ronnie cried.

"What can we do?" I asked.

"Can't we swim to them and bring them back here with us?"

"I think that would be too dangerous," I said. "We might get swept past them if we tried to swim to them, and I don't think we stand a chance trying to swim back to the dresser against this current."

"Maybe we could swim to them and hang onto their doghouse with them until the helicopter comes," Ronnie said.

"I suppose we could try that," I said, although I admit, I did not relish the idea.

Still, my heart went out to the two kids and I certainly didn't want to look like a coward. The little girl was probably about six years old and reminded me of Grace. She was thin and had stringy blond hair and she wore a flannel nightgown. The little boy was somewhat chubby, also blonde-haired and wore nothing more than cotton underwear. Both kids were shivering uncontrollably. I wondered how much longer they would last - not long without help, I was sure.

Ronnie's suggestion to swim over to the two kids might be possible. If we could somehow reach the kids maybe we could hold them in our arms and keep them warm until the helicopter picked us up. That might be their only hope for survival. The risk seemed enormous. I couldn't believe I was even thinking about doing this. I prayed big time.

"Oh Jesus, we need your help, please. Thank you for protecting Ronnie and me and those little kids. Thank you for bringing someone to rescue us soon."

I took Ronnie's hand and looked at her.

"You really want to do this?" I asked.

"I do," she said.

"Okay," I said, tying my red jacket around my waist in case I needed to throw it to the children as a life line. "Let's go then."

But just as we started to swim away from the dresser, a thought occurred to me."Wait!" I said. "Let's not let go of the dresser yet, let's try paddling our feet hard and steering over to those kids. If we can maneuver the dresser close enough, we can grab them. If we can't get close enough at least we'll be closer than we are now."

"Good idea," Ronnie said.

We began paddling our feet furiously. It didn't take much effort to propel the dresser forward in the rapid current. A major problem with our tactics became quickly apparent, however. It looked almost certain that we were going too fast and that we were going to ram the two little kids.

"Francis!" Ronnie yelled.

"I see," I yelled. "Let go of the dresser and try to push it off course."

Ronnie and I let go of the dresser and pushed as hard as we could to change its bearing. We succeeded in keeping it from hitting the kids, but now the two of us were adrift in the river. I tried to swim to the kids and their doghouse and to keep my eye on Ronnie.

"Francis, I can't make it," Ronnie screamed.

"I'll get you Ronnie," I said.

"Save the children," Ronnie yelled.

I frantically looked toward the riverbank for help. I didn't see anybody there. I scanned the sky for the helicopter. I didn't see it. I didn't see a boat either. And the girl I loved was fast being swept downriver out of my sight, maybe out of my life. Forever.

"I am with you," a voice said.

"Ronnie!" I screamed.

Just then the dog house that the kids were holding onto hit a partially submerged log. The jolt threw them into the roiling river. They screamed again for help.

"Save the children, Francis!" Ronnie called to me. "Save the children."

I prayed as hard as I'd ever prayed in my life.

"Jesus please help. Don't let Ronnie drown," I begged. "I'll do anything you want, just please don't let her drown."

"I am with you," a voice said.

Then I made my fateful promise. I vowed I would even become a priest if Jesus would save Ronnie. If I had to give up my dream of becoming a major league baseball player and someday marrying her to keep her alive, that's what I would do. I looked at my red jacket desperately seeking courage.

The two little kids were screaming non-stop. I managed to toss one arm of my jacket to the little girl. She grabbed hold of it and I reeled her in like a fish.

I caught hold of her by her nightgown and hung on to her. It was all I could do to keep from panicking, but I managed to remember reading somewhere once that most people who drowned did so because they failed to remain calm. Besides, there was that voice, "I am with you."

Still, the river was freezing cold, I was struggling to keep my head above the water, my legs felt really tired and the little girl was wriggling around in my arms like a wet squid.

"Stop squirming," I pleaded with her. "You'll make us drown."

Just then I spied her brother popping up to the surface a couple of feet away and gasping for air. It looked like he'd gone under once or twice already and this might be his last chance. I summoned what little strength I had left and swam close enough to the little boy to toss him the other arm of my jacket and reeled him in with my free hand. When he reached me, he grabbed hold of me in total panic and took all three of us under.

Both kids struggled to wriggle free of my grip, but I hung on to them and kicked us back up to the surface. When we broke water, I gulped a lung full of air and decided I was going to make it to shore or die trying. Ronnie was nowhere to be seen. I couldn't believe she was gone.

I didn't want to believe Ronnie was gone. Part of me wanted to let go of the two little kids and go try to find her. Part of me wanted to be done with this struggle and just drown. Part of me wanted to survive. I felt miserable, but I guess I still had some will to survive.

I decided to paddle toward the river bank. I realized then that my red jacket would interfere with my efforts, so I reluctantly let go of it and it floated away, I hoped my grandma would forgive me for losing it. I wondered if letting go of the jacket also meant I would lose Jesus' protection.

If I let go of Jesus would he let go of me in return?

Would I hear the voice saying, "I am with you," anymore? I didn't know. Letting go of Jesus and losing his protection, would be a really bad way to start out in the priesthood. Fortunately or unfortunately, I didn't have time to dwell on that thought very long.

I had to allow the current to take me downstream where it wanted to, but I also tried to cut diagonally across the current as much as I could, hoping that I would eventually wind up on shore. I kicked and fought and struggled to stay afloat and to hang on to the two kids. I don't know how long I struggled. After what feltlike an eternity in the freezing river water, I decided I couldn't keep up the struggle. This was much worse than trying to make my way out of the tunnel. I was so tired.

As much as I wanted to survive, every fiber of my being was screaming, "Give it up. You're lost. Ronnie's lost. Your life is over."

I let go of the two children and stopped paddling. I sank into the water. I welcomed death. It was kind of blissful to end things this way actually. I was okay with drowning after all. It would never have been my first choice for a way to die, but then who said we got to pick? Really, this wasn't bad. At least I wouldn't have to struggle any longer.

I saw Jesus waiting for me in the forest again. He was smiling benevolently at me. I fully intended to lay my head on his lap this time. I was so exhausted. I really needed to rest. Then my knees scraped something. At first I wasn't sure. But then it happened again.

Rocks! The river bottom. We had drifted close enough to shore to touch bottom. Despite incredible weariness, I forced myself to stand up. It was true! The water was only waist high here. I pulled the little girl and the little boy out of the water and dragged them to shore and collapsed on a sand bar. I never wanted to move again. I was so worn out I didn't think I could.

I don't know how long I laid there. After awhile I felt hands reaching out to me. They were gentle, like the hands of Jesus. Huh? Jesus looked just like Uncle Benny.

CHAPTER XV

A twelve-foot tall Christmas tree, twinkling with lights and decorated with paper chains, popcorn chains, and ornaments handcrafted by the kids at Blessed Redeemer Catholic Church's elementary school, stood near the altar. A gold star topped the tree. Gaily wrapped packages littered the floor beneath its branches. Everything was so beautiful, but Christmas was such a sad time to die.

The congregation was singing, "I am the resurrection and the life, saith the Lord; he that believeth in me, though he were dead, yet shall he live; and whosoever liveth and believeth in me shall never die."

The priest, the altar boys, and various lay people who would assist in the mass, proceeded up the center aisle to the altar. As they progressed forward, the priest swung a brass censer, also called a thurible, attached to a chain, from side to side. The exotic aroma of cedarwood incense smoldered out of the censer holes like a sweet smoke boiling out of my grandpa's pipe.

It must be Midnight Mass! But no! The priest was announcing he would be performing The Burial of the Dead, Rite One. Burial of the Dead? In Red vestments? At Midnight Mass? Weird.

The priest addressed the congregation soberly saying, "The grace of our Lord Jesus Christ and the love of God and the fellowship of the Holy Spirit be with you all."

The congregation responded saying, "And also with you."

Then the priest said, "O God, whose beloved Son did take little children into his arms and bless them: Give us grace, we beseech thee, to entrust this child, Francis Albert Forsyth to thy never-failing care and love, and bring us all to thy heavenly kingdom; through the same thy Son Jesus Christ Our Lord, who liveth and reigneth with thee and the Holy Spirit, one God, now and forever, Amen."

Francis Albert Forsyth? That was me! This wasn't Christmas Eve Midnight Mass. This was my funeral mass. No wonder I felt disconnected. Had Ronnie and I both died?

"God is our hope and strength, a very present help in trouble," the priest said. "Therefore we will not fear, though the earth be moved, and though the hills be carried into the midst of the sea; though the waters thereof rage and swell and though the mountains shake at the tempest of the same. There is a river, the streams whereof make glad the city of God, the holy place of the tabernacle of the Most Highest."

Just then my mom let out a loud howl of sorrow.

"My boy, my precious boy," she wailed.

"Precious boy?"

I was touched. Shocked, actually. My mom considered me precious? She coulda' fooled me.

I took the opportunity while grandpa and grandma quieted mom down to look around the crowded assemblage for Ronnie's parents. The sight of Ronnie being carried downstream in the swift current of the flooding MacKenzie River was still fresh in my mind. I was sure I would never see her again. Strange though, that the priest hadn't mentioned Ronnie's name, only mine. Maybe the Mailers didn't want her funeral service held at the same time as mine.

I looked some more for Doctor and Mrs. Mailer. Grandpa had told me they usually sat in the second or third row of pews in the center section of the church. People were such creatures of habit the Mailers probably were seated in their usual place. But to my dismay, I did not see them. I reasoned with myself that it was because the auditorium was set up differently than the church would have been and because there were so many people attending this mass. A lot of people were attending my funeral mass. That was cool.

Then the priest said, "In sure and certain hope of the resurrection to eternal life through our Lord Jesus Christ, we commend to the Almighty God our brother Francis Albert Forsyth; and we commit his body to the ground; earth to earth, ashes to ashes, dust to dust."

Dust fell on my face.

"Ronnie," I moaned. "Ronnie." I hoped I would be with her in heaven. But maybe she hadn't died.

My heart felt like somebody had tightened a steel cable around it and two eighteen-wheeler trucks were pulling it apart. Now the feeling really was physical, and it hurt a lot more than the rheumatic fever. If Ronnie was dead I was glad to be dead too.

"Ronnie's fine," Jesus – who looked like Uncle Benny – told me.

I spit the dust out of my mouth. If Ronnie was okay I wanted to be okay. I opened my eyes to see two rescue guys and Uncle Benny hovering over me, scolding the little boy and girl I had dragged out of the river for throwing sand on me.

Later, Doctor Mailer hovered over me too.

"Ronnie's fine," he assured me.

"She's not dead?" I asked, looking into the doctor's eyes for signs of sadness or lying to spare me. "It's a miracle," Doctor Mailer said grinning broadly, "but she's not dead and you're not dead,"

Behind Dr. Mailer I could see my mom, grandma and grandpa, Jeannie, Gizzie and my brothers and sisters.

"Where am I?" I asked.

"You're at the hospital."

"I'm not staying in a hospital again!" I insisted furiously. Unfortunately, my body did not respond at all to my effort to sit up and jump out of bed.

"Relax Francis," Doctor Mailer said. "You're beat up and you need some rest, but you're going to be okay and we'll have you out of here in no time."

"You swear?"

"I swear. You are very brave Francis," Doctor Mailer said patting me on the shoulder and beaming another big smile at me. "I want you to know that Mrs. Mailer and I appreciate very much what you did for Veronica."

"Your wife is okay too?" I said.

Doctor Mailer took my hand and squeezed it hard. "Mrs. Mailer's okay," he said as tears welled up in his eyes. "And you are an exceptional young man."

"Where's Web?" I asked.

"I'm sorry. Web didn't make it," Doctor Mailer said quietly.

I heard my mom moan in the background. I thought she didn't moan as loudly for him as she had for me at my funeral service, but that might have been wishful thinking. I was sorry for my mom, but I have to admit, even though I felt somewhat guilty for thinking it, I wasn't all that sorry about Web.

Then, I heard a sweet voice call my name!

"Francis!"

"Ronnie?"

"I'm here Francis," Ronnie said.

She called to me from a wheelchair as a nurse pushed the wheelchair into my room. When Ronnie reached my bedside she took my hand, rubbed it against her cheek and kissed it.

"I'm here Francis," she said. "We made it."

"We made it? But how?"

Ronnie told me how the helicopter pilot that we had seen earlier plucked her out of the river.

"I thought I was a good swimmer," she said. "But if that pilot hadn't come along when he did, I don't know."

"I am so glad he found you," I said. "Hey! What day is it?"

"It's Christmas Eve day," Ronnie said. "Sleep now if you want to. That's what I'm going to do. We can talk later."

"Sleep is the last thing I want," I said. "I'll only sleep if I know we still have a date to attend Midnight Mass together."

"Nothing could keep me from attending Midnight Mass with you tonight," Ronnie assured me. "I'm wearing my new dress so you better be there."

"I'll be there," I promised.

Ronnie leaned over and kissed me on the cheek. Doctor Mailer must have given me some powerful drugs then, because I promptly drifted off to la-la land and didn't wake up again until after supper time.

"Let's see," Doctor Mailer said, holding my wrist and taking my pulse. "We checked you in here around eight this morning and it's now eight in the evening. You think twelve hours of rest is going to be enough for you?"

"That's plenty."

"Can you get out of bed and stand on your own two feet?"

I swung my feet out of bed and stood up. I felt a little woozy, but tried not to show it.

"You still look a little shaky," Doctor Mailer said, "But it is Christmas Eve and I think the best medicine I can prescribe for you now is to let you out of here. Besides, I'm not letting you take my daughter to church until you go home and clean up."

"Go home with your grandpa here, take a bath, get something to hot to eat and you'll be just fine."

"Thanks Doctor Mailer!" I said.

I wanted to let out a whoop of joy, but figured I might disturb the other patients. Doctor Mailer checked me out of the hospital and grandpa drove me home. On the way home I noticed that it had finally quit raining.

EPILOGUE

The temperature continued to drop that evening and by the time grandpa drove us all to church for Midnight Mass, it was snowing. The world looked fresh and new under its shimmering blanket of white. I thought of *Silent Night* again and thanked God that I was still alive to experience the incredible beauty of his world.

Ronnie met me at the front of the church. She was dressed in a simple red taffeta dress with a white shawl around her shoulders. Her hair shined and she radiated beauty like a Christmas angel. I was glad she was not an angel though. I was glad she was real, and we were sitting together close to the front of the auditorium. We held hands as Father Shanahan announced that the special occasion we were celebrating that evening was the birth of our Lord and Savior Jesus Christ. I can't tell you how relieved I was that the special occasion was not the Burial of the Dead for Francis Albert Forsyth.

Father Shanahan prayed over the holy water, "Lord God Almighty, creator of all life, of body and soul, we ask you to bless this water: as we use it in faith. Forgive our sins and save us from all illness and the power of evil. Lord, in your mercy give us living water, always springing up as a fountain of salvation: free us, body and soul, from every danger, and admit us to your presence in purity of heart. Grant this through Christ our Lord, amen."

"Amen," said the congregation.

"My brothers and sisters," Father Shanahan said, "to prepare ourselves to celebrate the sacred mysteries, let us call to mind our sins."

"Lord, we have sinned against you: Lord have mercy."

"Lord, have mercy," the congregation replied.

"Lord, show us your mercy and love. And grant us your salvation."

"May almighty God have mercy on us, forgive us our sins and bring us to everlasting life."

"Amen."

Then the nuns, who were seated in a special section off to the right of everybody else led us in chanting the *kyrie eleison* several times, which I think meant "Lord have mercy on us."

Father Shanahan performed the Rite of Blessing and Sprinkling of Holy Water while we chanted, moving through the congregation sprinkling the holy water on as many people as he possibly could.

"Dear friends," he said, "this water will be used to remind us of our baptism. Let us ask God to bless it, and to keep us faithful to the Spirit he has given us."

I confess I wasn't quite sure I wanted to be blessed with water at that point, after what I'd been through in the river. But I decided it was okay. I was safe and I was going to be safe now for a long, long time. I felt convinced of that.

Father Shanahan repeated, "Lord have mercy."

Then we were done chanting and I thought it was pretty appropriate to ask for mercy after the way we had crucified the *kyrie*. Then the nuns led us in singing the *Gloria*, which we messed up about as badly as the *kyrie*. The words "Glory to God in the highest, and peace to his people on earth," just seemed to lose something in translation between the *Daily Missal* and our mouths. Father Shanahan then led us in another short prayer while we kneeled in front of our chairs.

Fortunately, the janitor, Mr. Chavez, and his crew had installed portable kneeling pads in front of the chairs. The cement floor of the auditorium would have been pretty hard to kneel on.

After that prayer, we all sat down for the First Reading of the Word, followed by the Responsorial Psalm and the Second Reading of the Word. We stood again for the Gospel Acclamation and reading of the Gospel and the Homily and the Profession of Faith.

We recited the words of The Nicene Creed. The Prayer of the Faithful and the General Intercession passed quickly. Father Shanahan's short sermon, which was in Latin and hard to understand anyway, ended quickly. Then Father Shanahan began to prepare for communion.

I especially liked communion. It made me feel cleansed and refreshed to partake of the bread and wine. I was especially grateful to be participating in this communion after my near drowning. The wine was the real stuff too. It wasn't grandpa's, but it was good nonetheless. At least it was not watered-down grape juice.

I liked it that the Roman Catholic Church encouraged people to consistently re-bond with Christ through the quiet ritual of communion. My grandma had explained to me that Roman Catholics saw communion as nourishment for the spirit, whereas Protestants seemed to prize loud praying, singing, jumping up and down and making a spectacle of oneself as the way to achieve closeness to God.

All I knew was I felt better when I practiced the quiet personal act of walking up to the altar and taking communion than I ever did shouting "Praise Jesus" and waving my hands in the air so everybody could see how connected to the Holy Spirit I was. On this night, I felt especially close to Jesus and God, and the Roman Catholic Church. Nobody, not even my mom was going to be able to make a Protestant out of me now.

A layperson poured wine from a ceramic pitcher into a gold-plated chalice. Father Shanahan launched into presentation of the gifts saying, "Blessed are you, Lord God of all creation. Through your goodness we have this bread to offer, which earth has given and human hands have made. It will become for us the bread of life."

"Blessed be God forever," the congregation responded.

The altar server took the "bread," which consisted of thin white wafers, out of the Ciborium, another gold-plated cup, and placed them on two patens or small plates.

Father Shanahan said, "Pray my brothers and sisters, that our sacrifice may be acceptable to God, the almighty Father."

"May the Lord accept the sacrifice at your hands, for the praise and glory of his name, for our good, and the good of all the Church," the congregation responded.

Father Shanahan said a prayer over the communion elements then led the congregation into the Eucharist itself.

"The Lord be with you."

"And also with you," we responded.

"Lift up your hearts."

"We lift them up to the Lord."

"Let us give thanks to the Lord, our God."

"It is right to give him thanks and praise."

"It is right that we should give thanks unto thee oh Lord," Father Shanahan said. "Therefore with Angels and Archangels, and with all the company of heaven, we laud and magnify thy glorious Name; evermore praising thee, and saying . . ."

The congregation butchered another responsive chant: "Holy, Holy, Holy Lord, God of power and might. Heaven and Earth are full of thy glory. Hosanna in the highest. Blessed is he who comes in the name of the Lord."

"Hosanna in the highest."

"Lord, by your death on the cross and resurrection, you have set us free," Father Shanahan continued. "You are the light of the world."

"Amen."

"Through him, with him, and in him, in the unity of the Holy Spirit, all glory and honor is yours, almighty Father, for ever and ever."

"Amen."

Father Shanahan then led us in reciting the Lord's Prayer. When we finished he said, "Deliver us Lord, from every evil, and grant us peace in our day. In your mercy keep us free from sin and protect us from all anxiety as we wait in joyful hope for the coming of our Savior, Jesus Christ."

"For the kingdom, the power, and the glory are yours, now and forever," the congregation responded.

"Lord Jesus, you said to your apostles: I leave you peace, my peace I give you. Look not on our sins, but on the faith of your Church, and grant us the peace and unity of your kingdom where you live for ever and ever."

"Amen."

Father Shanahan made the sign of the cross and said, "The Peace of the Lord be with you always."

"And also with you," we responded.

At that point Father Shanahan urged the members of the congregation to greet each other, offering each other peace. I turned to Ronnie. She looked deeply into my eyes and said, "Peace to you Francis."

I put my arms around her, held her close and said, "Peace to you too Ronnie." Then I whispered "I love you," into her fragrant brown hair. She clutched me tightly.

"I love you too," She said.

When the congregation sat down Father Shanahan held the bread and wine aloft and said, "This is the Lamb of God who takes away the sins of the world. Happy are those who are called to his supper."

We responded, "Lord, I am not worthy to receive you, but only say the word and I shall be healed."

At that point, people started to leave their seats and shuffle toward the altar. My legs felt tired and a little shaky when I stood up, but I managed to wobble toward the altar without falling down. I felt several hands reach out to steady me as I made my way forward; kind hands; hands of people who cared about me. My heart filled with gladness. My eyes filled with tears. Father Shanahan had been right about everybody in the parish being his family and how much love they could give.

I watched people in line in front of me sticking out their tongues or holding up their hands to receive the communion wafers. I decided I would hold out my hand. When I reached the altar, a woman layperson dressed in a white robe, placed a thin white wafer in my hands and said, "The Body of Christ."

To which I muttered, "Amen."

As I walked toward the layperson with the wine cup I looked at Ronnie standing in front of me and I thanked Jesus again for the protection of my red jacket. Then I remembered my promise.

"I vowed that I would become a priest if you saved Ronnie," I said. I was a little hesitant to take such a big step, but to my surprise, I actually wanted to.

"You will not be held to your vow," Jesus said.

"But I meant it," I said, and a sense of quiet confidence came over me.

"I know you meant it," Jesus said. "But because you were willing, without thought for your own safety, to give up your life for Veronica and for those two children, and because you are willing to obey the call of our Father, you will not be held to your vow."

"If you want to become a priest, we will welcome you with open arms. If you choose not to, you will still be blessed among men. You are a true disciple of the faith Francis Albert Forsyth."

I reached the layperson with the wine cup. He blessed me.

As I drank from the cup I swear I heard angles singing Handel's magnificent *Hallelujah Chorus*

"For the Lord God Omni-Potent Reigneth. Hallelujah! Hallelujah! Hallelujah!"

I didn't know if I was going to become a baseball player or a priest, or something else. But it didn't matter on this Christmas Eve because I was alive and I still had time to think about it

"The Lord reigneth indeed, I thought. "Hallelujah!"

I was born again! The old Francis Albert Forsyth was gone. In his place was somebody new; somebody I suddenly realized I liked a lot and really wanted to get to know.

THE END